More Sandy Shorts

Stories set in and around Rehoboth, Bethany, Lewes,
Fenwick Island, Cape May, and Chincoteague

Nancy Powichroski Sherman

Cat & Mouse Press
Lewes, DE 19958
www.catandmousepress.com

Published by Cat & Mouse Press
Lewes, DE, 19958
www.catandmousepress.com

ISBN: 978-1-7323842-3-1

Cover illustration by Patti Shreeve
Cover illustration Copyright © 2018 Patti Shreeve
Author photo by Carolyn Watson Photography

Printed in the United States of America

"Maybe We Will" was previously published online by *Fox Chase Review*, Summer 2015, in an earlier version titled "Saving the Child."

Dedication

This collection of short stories is dedicated to:

My husband Matthew

...that I love you.

In memoriam for:

Leonard and Lillian Powichroski,

my parents,

who introduced me to the Atlantic Ocean.

Contents

Acknowledgements

I would like to thank:

Nancy Day Sakaduski

> for the supportive environment she creates as both an editor and publisher. Working with her feels like a collaboration more than a publisher/author relationship. When I pitched my first collection, *Sandy Shorts*, she took a chance on me, and I am grateful to be part of the Cat & Mouse Press family. I admire her dedication to the writing community through her yearly Rehoboth Beach Reads Short Story Contest, her webpage—*Cat & Mouse Press: A Playful Publisher*, and her e-newspaper—*Writing is a Shore Thing*.

Linda Chambers

> for encouraging me as a writer, for copyediting my drafts, but mostly for being my BFF and beach adventure sister.

Maribeth Fischer

> for establishing the Rehoboth Beach Writers Guild and helping me hone my skills as a storyteller.

Matthew Woodward Sherman

> for being supportive and understanding concerning the amount of time I spend writing on my computer.

And all the wonderful people who answered my phone calls and offered information as I did my research on the places, events, and activities used in these stories.

Works Hard for Her Money

"Don't touch that, Cody!" Grace grabbed the eight-year-old's hand before he could pull the bar of the emergency alarm on the parking-level wall of the Cape May-Lewes ferry.

"I'm not Cody!" the boy insisted. "I'm Jody."

Grace took note of the stripes on the boy's shirt and those on the shirt of his identical twin. Switching identities was their favorite trick but, as their nanny, she had long ago figured out the key: Cody's clothing was usually in his favorite color, blue, and Jody's was usually green. "No. You're Cody, Mr. Blue Stripes." The boy's face puckered with displeasure at being outsmarted.

Though Grace now had Cody restrained, the challenge was not over; another small hand reached for the lever. "Stop it, Jody!" She pulled the other boy's hand away from the alarm. Then, with the twin boys in tow, she led the way to the main passenger area on the second floor of the ferry and seated them in a booth by the windows.

Only eighty-five minutes until freedom, she chanted silently in her mind. In little over an hour, she would turn over her two charges to their grandparents, who would spoil them for two weeks at their Cape May home before delivering the little brats to Goose Rocks Academy for

Boys in Kennebunkport, Maine, where the twins would experience their first year of boarding school. Grace wondered if the headmaster and teachers were prepared for these unruly identicals.

"I'm thirsty!"

"Me, too!"

Grace expected difficulties throughout this trip from Lewes, Delaware, to Cape May, New Jersey, but she was counting on this table with a view of the bay to keep the boys distracted from their usual mischiefs.

"Stay here. I'm giving you both a great responsibility: Your jobs are to guard this booth so no one else takes it while I get you drinks from the food court." She pointed to where she would be going. "That's the food court. I'll be keeping an eye on you. Don't leave the booth for any reason."

"But what if the ferry starts to sink?" Cody asked.

"I guess you'll have to go down with the ship just like a ship's captain is expected to do."

Grace walked sideways, knowing she probably looked foolish, but also knowing that she'd better keep her eyes on the Dowell twins. Inside the food court, she bypassed the soda fountain and, with her eyes still focused on the twins, she grabbed two juice boxes. But then she made a major mistake: She decided to pour a small, black coffee for herself. When she looked back at the booth, only Jody was still seated there.

She stood tall to see if Cody was hiding down in the seat. No luck. She rushed toward the cashier and handed her a ten-dollar bill. "Keep the change."

"You forgot to get this." Cody stood behind her, holding

up an extra-large cup of cola.

Grace took the cup from Cody's hand and gave it to the cashier. "I assume that the ten will cover this, too. If you like cola, it's all yours." With the juice boxes safe in the side pocket of her purse and her coffee firm in one hand, she grabbed Cody's hand with her other.

"I hate you," he said.

She looked down at him with a tight smile. "No problem. In just a little bit of time, you won't have to listen to me anymore." When she looked up, Jody was no longer guarding the booth; it was now occupied by a young couple. "There was a little boy sitting here, this one's twin brother. Did you see where he went?"

The young man's eyebrows pushed together. "No lo entiendo."

Grace sighed. She had taken French in high school. This was definitely not French. Still, she gave it a try. "Avez-vous voir où le petit garçon est allé?" Seeing the look of confusion on their faces, she tried acting it out. She pointed to Cody, then pointed to the booth, then shrugged, then pointed in two different directions, and shrugged again.

She watched as the young lady's eyes registered understanding. "¡Sí!" She pointed toward the back of the ferry and made the gesture of opening a door.

"Merci. I mean, thank you."

"Gracias," Cody corrected her. Grace had forgotten that the boys had studied Spanish in pre-K. And though she didn't take those classes with them (one of the few times each day she had to herself), she didn't need a Spanish lesson to translate his next words, "Ella es un idiota."

She repeated, "Gracias," to the couple, and with hope

that she might adapt Cody's insult accurately, she pointed to Cody and added, "El es un idiota."

The young couple laughed, so she knew she had succeeded. She tossed her full coffee cup into a trash can and dragged Cody down the aisle. "What's the plan, Cody? Where did Jody go?"

Cody glared at her. "How should I know? I'm just an idiota."

"This is serious, Cody. Someone could kidnap your brother."

"That's okay with me. I don't want a twin, anyway."

She said the first thing that popped into her mind. "You shouldn't say that. Someday, you might need one of his kidneys."

The sky was cloudy, and a brisk wind and agitated waves from a distant tropical storm rocked the ferry more than usual, sending saltwater spray onto the deck and benches. Consequently, the back deck was empty. Grace had mixed feelings about this situation. She was disappointed that there was no one who might have seen Jody, but she was also relieved that the unpleasant weather would drive Jody back into the interior of the ferry and, therefore, safe from falling overboard as the boat swayed in the rough water.

But what if Jody didn't heed the danger? What if he did something stupid like sit on the thick metal chain that closed the ends of the ferry's lower level? Then, for a brief second, she allowed herself the image of Jody doing the dog paddle across the Delaware Bay in the wake of the boat. And for a slightly longer second, she added Cody next to him. But the reality of the situation destroyed its humor, and Grace, with Cody in tow, looked for help.

As they rounded the corner to other side of the boat, she saw the back of a giant, blue, cartoonish pirate character, standing by the railing.

Cody pulled his hand from hers and rushed forward. "Lighthouse Pete!" he called out, just before he slipped on the metal deck and slid forward in an uncontrolled trajectory.

"Oh my God!" Grace screamed. Her fears of boy overboard sent panic throughout her body. She ran toward the fallen boy in uneven steps as the boat swayed.

The tall mascot of the Cape May-Lewes Ferry heard the commotion and turned toward them. He reached his hand down to Cody, and when the boy stood, the blue furry-suited Lighthouse Pete the Pirate pretended to dust him off.

Another young voice squealed, "Lighthouse Pete!" from behind a large metal box labeled "Life Preservers: 50 adult, 50 children." Jody rushed out, dragging two backpacks, his and Cody's.

The mascot waved him over and wrapped his arms around both boys in a hug that made Grace consider taking a cell phone picture to send to their parents. Then, it occurred to her that this wouldn't be her job much longer.

Lighthouse Pete opened the door and gestured for them to go inside the passenger area of the ferry. As Grace entered the doorway with the twins, the mascot bowed to her and pretended to tip his pirate hat.

The dampness outside had sent all the passengers indoors, so the area by the food court was packed, but Grace managed to find a half-booth, a one-seater, at the far end of the aisle near the gift shop. Perfect. It meant corralling the boys into the seat, with her at the only escapable end. She produced the two apple-juice boxes from her purse, hoping to keep the boys occupied and give her a moment of quiet.

An auburn-haired woman in a ferry-crew shirt approached the table and handed Grace a fresh cup of coffee. "A gift from an admirer."

Grace looked around but didn't notice anyone looking in her direction. A moment later, she heard a tap on the window. Lighthouse Pete waved through the glass. The boys waved back. The mascot waved again, but this time he pointed to Grace.

Both boys glared at her. Cody called her rude, and Jody snapped, "He's waiting for you to wave back."

Grace waved back, and the mascot bowed and touched the tip of his hat. Then, he disappeared down the deck. Cody tried to climb over Jody to see where Lighthouse Pete had gone, but Jody pushed back. "He's already gone, stupid."

Grace sipped her coffee and thought of how different tomorrow would be for her. Five years as a nanny for the Dowell family felt like fifty. Every night, she checked her natural honey-blonde hair for any sign of gray. None so far, thank goodness. She looked at her watch. Forty-five more minutes until docking at the Cape May terminal, where Grandfather and Grandmother Dowell would be waiting for them.

Unfortunately, delivering the twins to their grandparents also meant being out of work. In coastal Delmarva, most of the families who might seek a nanny were summer people, and Grace couldn't afford to work only during the beach season. Admittedly, she could use her degree in early childhood education to seek a job in the public-school system but working with the twins had extinguished her love of teaching.

Grace studied the travelers seated nearby and played guess-the-occupation. Lawyer. Doctor. Yoga instructor. Truck driver. Retiree. Hair stylist. Tax accountant. Of course, these were only guesses. Clothing and deportment aren't always indicative of one's career.

A juice box with the hand still attached appeared in front of her face. "Grace, I'm done."

She grabbed the juice box before it could be squeezed to send sticky juice down her blouse, another favorite trick of the twins. "*Miss* Grace, Cody." She hated that the Dowells let their kids call her by her first name, so she corrected them on every occasion. "And you're not *done*; you're *finished*. Use the right word."

A second juice box slid past Cody and fell off the edge of the table. "I'm done, too. And I gotta go to the bathroom," Jody announced.

"Me, too. Me, too. I gotta pee." Cody's voice was embarrassingly loud.

A quick glance showed Grace where the restrooms were located, not far from their half-booth. She considered reminding the twins of the difference between a *bathroom* and a *restroom*, but the previous teachable moment about *done* vs. *finished* had been a waste of time, and the kids would be out of her life upon arrival at Cape May, so she decided to save her breath and simply get the boys to the men's restroom.

"I'll hold your backpacks."

The boys ignored her and rushed into the restroom with their backpacks still on their shoulders.

The coffee she had just drunk was demanding that she

slip into the women's restroom. She looked inside only long enough to determine that the line was too long and decided she couldn't risk losing one or both of the twins. She leaned her back against the wall and aimed her eyes at the door to the men's restroom to be sure that neither of the Dowell boys could sneak out.

The door opened, and a green-striped twin exited. "Over here, Jody."

Surprisingly, the boy joined her without protest or incident.

After numerous men and young boys entered and exited the restroom, Grace looked down at her watch. Ten minutes had passed. "Jody, go back in and check on your brother."

The boy practically skipped to the door and disappeared inside. A moment later, a blue-striped Cody joined her at the wall.

"Great! Now I have you, Cody, but why isn't your brother with you?"

The boy shrugged. "Because Jody's not in there, duh."

"I saw your brother go in to get you. He didn't come back out. So, what are you two up to?"

"Nothing. Maybe he got flushed down the toilet and into the bay." She noticed the grin creeping over his face. She also noticed a bit of green striped fabric peaking from the partially zipped compartment of his backpack. "This isn't funny, Jody!"

On hearing his correct name, Jody's face reddened.

Grace held tightly to Jody's arm as she asked a blue-shirted crew member to check the men's restroom for a young boy who might be shirtless. She pointed to Jody's face. "He'll look just like this one."

"I know," the crew member said, as he bowed and tipped a non-existent hat.

Grace recognized the gesture. Could this guy be Lighthouse Pete the Pirate? Unlike the cartoon character, this guy was a stunningly handsome thirty-something guy with light-brown hair and hazel eyes. His muscular shoulders stretched his shirt and his arms were dark tan from working on the water.

The crew member walked into the restroom to check for Cody and returned just as quickly. "He's not in there." He stooped down to be face-to-face with Jody. "Young man, this is not a good time or place to play games like this. Where is your brother?"

Jody, in his usual attempt to distract, pointed to a badge on the crewman's shirt. "What's ABS mean?"

"Able-Bodied Seaman."

"But this isn't a sea; it's a bay," Jody said, with a smirk on his face. "Why aren't you an Able-Bodied Bay Man?"

The crew member ignored the challenge. "Regardless of job title, I have the responsibility to protect the ferry in any situation, even when that situation is created by two misbehaving children." He winked at Grace, then towered over the boy. "It is my duty to take such children to the brig."

Jody shifted feet several times. "It was Cody's idea."

"And where is your brother hiding?"

"I don't know. He gave me his shirt and then left."

In those ten seconds that she had glanced into the women's room, Cody had escaped? She shook her head in disbelief.

The crew member activated his walkie-talkie. "ABS Garrison here, second floor, by the restrooms. We have a missing child. Wavy black hair. Brown eyes. Navy cargo shorts. Black Teva sandals. Possibly shirtless." He stared into Jody's eyes. "Shirtless?"

After an uncomfortable moment, the young boy gave in. "No, he's wearing his *Star Wars* T-shirt."

"Did you hear that? A *Star Wars* T-shirt." Then Garrison added the final detail. "Carrying an Eddie Bauer backpack."

Grace added, "And he's eight years old."

Garrison repeated, "And he's eight years old. His name is Cody…"

"Dowell."

"Cody Dowell. Got it?" Then, the crew member asked Grace, "Dowell of B.T. Dowell Technologies?"

She nodded. "That's right."

A button on the walkie-talkie lit up and a voice crackled through. "Already have a sighting. Just got a call from the food court. The description sounds like the little thief who rushed out with an armful of chips and cookies. Langley is already in pursuit."

"Cookies?" Jody stomped his foot. "He'd better save some for me." He plopped on the floor and hid his face in his crossed arms.

ABS Garrison lifted the boy to his feet. "You're coming with me to the captain's bridge. You and your brother are in big trouble."

"But I didn't steal anything. Cody's the thief."

Jody sniffled all the way to the bridge, but he didn't get any sympathy. When they arrived, the captain told Jody that he and his brother had endangered not only themselves but also everyone on board, as the crew had to leave their assigned posts to focus on finding his twin brother.

"And this isn't the only time they've done this today," Garrison said, but quickly added, "Lighthouse Pete told me the boys were playing hide-and-seek out on the deck in this rough crossing."

Grace smiled. She was right. ABS Garrison was Lighthouse Pete the Pirate.

The door opened and another crew member, who looked young enough to have just graduated from high school, entered with Cody, who was still clinging to the food he'd taken. "He refused to budge unless I let him bring his snacks," the young guy said.

Cody pointed to Grace. "She'll pay for it."

Grace reached into her purse. "How much do we owe the food court for all these chips and cookies?"

"Not a penny." The captain brought an empty box to Cody. "Drop them in here." After the boy did so, the captain tossed the box onto his desk. "These will be returned to the food court." Then, he stared into the eyes of the two boys. "As the captain of this ship, I have the authority to be your judge and to sentence you. I find you both guilty of misconduct, and I sentence you to be detained. ABS Langley will take you to the glass room and keep you there until we dock at Cape May," the captain said. "Now, everyone get out. I have a ferry to run."

ABS Langley used a thin bungee cord to fashion handcuffs and took Jody and Cody down the staircase. Both boys were pale and on the verge of crying. Grace started to follow them. "They'll be okay," Garrison said, walking beside her. "Mike is just acting the part."

"I can't let them out of my sight. Not until I hand them

over to their grandparents," she explained to him.

"The glass room is a video arcade. Mike will keep them occupied on the game machines."

"That's punishment?"

"At least they'll be contained and staying out of trouble."

Grace was doubtful. "They're little monsters. When they get tired of the games, they'll find a way to get past him."

He shook his head. "Not likely. Mike is a black belt in Taekwondo, and on weekends, he works with kids in a detention home, so he's used to dealing with difficult children." Then, he added. "I'm sorry. I shouldn't have called your kids difficult."

"My kids?" Grace laughed. "I'm not their mother, thank God. Although I'd love to have some of her clothing—all designer stuff that I'd appreciate more than she does. I work for the Dowells as a nanny."

"Nanny? So, maybe you're single?"

She liked where this might be going. "I am. Is Lighthouse Pete single?"

"That depends on which Lighthouse Pete you're talking about. I'm not the only crew member to don that suit. But if you're talking about me, this Lighthouse Pete— though I prefer being called Ben—is indeed single and very glad to hear that his damsel-in-distress is also single."

"Well, Ben, I've always dreamed of being a damsel, but I'm over the 'in distress' part."

They arrived at the arcade, where Mike Langley was removing the bungee cuffs from the boys.

Ben nodded in their direction. "Mike loves a challenge, especially when it involves helping kids straighten up."

Grace exhaled. "I'm happy to pass the little brats to their grandparents, who will most likely be relieved to hand them over to the headmaster at Goose Rocks Academy for Boys."

"A military academy?"

"Unfortunately, no. The Dowells find their children's antics amusing, even at the expense of their exhausted employees."

Ben smiled. "May I take this exhausted employee of the Dowell family to dinner while she's in Cape May?"

"This no-longer-exhausted, soon-to-be ex-employee of the Dowell family gladly accepts the invitation."

Ben stayed by her side until the boat docked, and he and Mike accompanied her as she took the twins to their awaiting grandparents, who hugged and kissed the boys as though they were sweet little angels.

As the Dowells left the terminal, Grace exhaled a long sigh. "My servitude is over."

Ben put his arm around her. "But your date has just begun."

She erased the entire Dowell family from her mind and began to anticipate a romantic dinner for two with her favorite able-bodied (beyond the maritime meaning) guy. She was looking forward to getting to know ABS Ben Garrison (no longer Lighthouse Pete) more intimately and wondered if there could ever be a Mrs. Lighthouse Pete the Pirate. Could her life be taking a turn for the better?

Shiver me timbers.

Between Worlds

What started as a routine day for Gina would soon turn into a mind-blowing experience that would make her question her sanity.

It happened on a Friday morning, the second week of June, known by locals as the last day before the official start of the summer season and the onslaught of vacationers. Although Gina had left her house at seven a.m. with Eddie, her four-year-old golden retriever, the traffic was already building into what would become "Traffic Gridlock Land" by noon.

It was too early in the day for the muscles in the back of her neck to already be tight, yet they were. Too much stress. She needed time on the beach this morning more than her dog did.

At a red light, she glanced at herself in the rearview mirror and saw a few more wrinkles around her eyes, accented by the dark circles under them. She couldn't believe how much she had aged in the past few months. Just last year, people had commented that she looked much younger than thirty-nine. They wouldn't say that now. Yesterday, she found a strand of gray peeking out from her chestnut-brown hair. She didn't notice that the light had turned green until a horn blasted by a pickup truck startled her.

She had a lot on her mind. A corporate takeover was

threatening her job security as the regional manager for Delmarva Swimsuits, especially because the founder and long-time president, sweet old Harry Chambers, had been "retired" during the takeover process. Gina, who had worked for the local company since she was eighteen, was trying her best to put out fires as she assured her sales staff at all fifteen locations that she was doing everything she could to keep their stores open, while she played word-dodgeball with their new boss, the president and CEO of American Beauty Swimwear, and his "executive assistant," Kelsea McNeil.

As Gina pulled her red Jeep Wrangler into a parking spot at Gordons Pond, she felt her tension melt away. Being near the ocean always did this for her. She turned off the ringer of her cell phone and inhaled the healing scent of salt air. "It's going to be a good day, Eddie." She donned her faded pink Rehoboth Beach baseball cap, attached a leash to Eddie's collar, and led her buddy over the dune and past the jetty to the area of beach that allowed dogs in the summer as long as they were leashed.

Since no one else was on the beach this early, she could ignore the leash-only rule for a while. She released Eddie, but the dog remained seated. "Are you waiting for this?" Gina removed a fluorescent green ball from her messenger bag and threw it down the beach.

She watched Eddie chase after the ball, his tail waving in the ocean breeze, the picture of pure joy. He retrieved the ball and then stood far off, waiting for her to come get it, a game he always played with Gina.

"Not happening, Eddie. Bring me the ball."

He sprinted toward her and dropped the ball at her feet.

Then, he sat again and waited for the next round.

"Good boy!" She ruffled his fur and gave him a hug. "You're just what I need this morning—an excuse to live in the moment."

Her phone vibrated. The number had a Florida area code. Carlson Barlow's office. "Damn!"

She stood up and threw the ball for Eddie again, then sat down on the sand. "Hello?"

The female voice on the other end had a recognizable attitude. It was McNeil. "Good morning, Ms. Winston. This is Kelsea McNeil, Mr. Barlow's EA calling you." As though her voice didn't already identify her.

Gina knew EA was the acronym for "executive assistant," but she preferred to think of it as standing for "epic asshole."

"Mr. Barlow is still waiting for the evaluations of your fifteen stores and the staff at each of them. His decision on which locations to close is dependent on your comments. At least so far. If he doesn't get that paperwork emailed by ten a.m. tomorrow, he'll just close eight stores at random and dismiss the staffs of those locations." Her voice made it clear that she'd have no problem firing people.

Gina held back her ire by forcing a smile. She had learned long ago that this was a method of bringing calmness to one's voice. "All the Delmarva Swimsuits stores are doing equally well."

McNeil cleared her throat. "You mean, American Beauty Swimwear? Delmarva Swimsuits no longer exists."

"Yes, of course. American Beauty Swimwear. It's difficult to erase from my mind the original company's name after working for them for more than twenty years." Gina wasn't sure whether she should continue, but she did. "Ms. McNeil …" It was difficult to even say that woman's name. "It's impossible for me to rate our salespeople. They're all top notch." She hated to suggest a possible solution but knew she had to offer something that could appease her new boss and yet be somewhat fair to the employees. "Maybe Mr. Barlow could save those who have the longest seniority."

"That, my dear, is an ineffectual way to keep a company going. If your salespeople are all equally qualified, then it would be better to keep the newer staff. They'll generally be younger, better at relating to the customers, and will adjust quickly to the changes ahead. Besides, the employees who have been there the longest will expect to continue at a higher pay level. Not good for our bottom line."

My dear? How dare this just-out-of-college epic ass-hole talk down to her? Gina was so furious she hung up. "Bitch!" She wished she had said that before hanging up, or that she'd actually called the woman an epic asshole, but name-calling wasn't going to improve the situation or help her stay employed as regional manager for the swimwear company. And she certainly needed to keep her job.

She stood, brushed the damp sand from her cropped jeans, and assumed a yoga tree pose, slowly inhaling the white cloud of good provided by the ocean, then exhaling the dark cloud of anger. It took ten exchanges of air to calm her. *At least she called while I'm here at my favorite part of the beach with my best pal, Eddie.*

One more inhale/exhale; then, she turned, to see how far her dog had run to catch the ball.

Eddie was nowhere in sight.

Her mind was confused. How could he not be there? "Eddie! Eddie!" she shouted, running down the beach toward the area where he should have been.

She scanned the ocean. No sign of Eddie, but the water was calm that morning so she felt that her golden retriever, with swimming in his DNA, would not have drowned.

If not in the ocean or on the beach, he must be among the sea grass that led to the trails of Henlopen State Park. Did Eddie get tired of waiting with the green ball in his mouth? Did he chase after something? Did he follow the scent of food from the campground?

Blades of sea grass scraped against her legs as she walked inland, calling his name over and over, each time in a slightly different direction.

She stood at the edge of a trail and asked joggers if they'd seen a golden retriever. All responded, "No. Sorry."

Gina ran back to the beach, still holding on to the possibility that she would be greeted with the sloppy dog kisses of her buddy. But her hopes were dashed. The beach was empty. She sank to the sand, covered her face with her hands, and cried.

Above her sobs, she heard the sound of a dog barking. Her heartbeat quickened. She looked up and saw two boys holding tightly to the collar of a chocolate Labrador retriever that was practically dragging them toward her.

"Hey, lady, is this your dog?" one of the boys asked. "We found him sniffing a tent down by our campsite. We were feeding him a hotdog when we heard you calling out the name on his collar—Eddie."

She shook her head. "No, that's not my Eddie. My dog is a golden retriever."

The Lab broke away from the boys and lay down in front of Gina.

"He sure acts like he's your dog," the other boy noted.

"That not possible. Sure, he's a retriever, but not the same breed."

"Well, our mom said we can't keep him, so if he's not yours, then I guess he'll have to find his own way home."

The boys left, but the Labrador remained in front of Gina.

Although she felt a tug of sorrow for this lost Labrador who shared a name with her golden retriever, her priority was to find *her* Eddie.

She walked toward the parking lot where her jeep was parked, but she was not alone. The Labrador followed behind her, then caught up to her, and then ran ahead. He jumped into the back seat, exactly where Eddie always sat.

Gina's eyes welled with tears. Even though this was not her dog, she couldn't abandon it. She would at least deliver the Lab to a park ranger and let the officials take it from there.

She reached down to connect the Lab's collar to the car's safety harness. Under the name Eddie, which was engraved on the metal ID, was a number that indicated the dog was microchipped, just like her golden. No need to drive to the park office. All she had to do to reunite this dog with its family would be to take him to the closest veterinarian and get him scanned. The result would provide a contact number to reach his owners.

She prayed that whoever found her Eddie would do the same.

Dr. Maycomb, the veterinarian who had recently opened Beach Pet Care, a new practice on Coastal Highway, scanned the dog and was delighted to share the results. "This Lab is indeed named Eddie, just as written on his collar. His owner is a woman named Gina Winston who lives at—"

Gina felt the blood drain from her face. "No! I'm Gina Winston, but he's not my dog. My Eddie is a four-year-old golden retriever."

Concern spread over the doctor's face. "If you're Gina Winston and live in Long Neck, this is your dog. Microchips don't lie."

"There must be a mistake in the database."

Dr. Maycomb's face clouded over. "Look, if this is some kind of ruse to dump your dog, your dramatics aren't necessary. I'll be glad to contact a shelter."

A shelter? But what if it's not a no-kill shelter? This Lab may not be her dog, but she wouldn't let it be sent off to wait in a cage until adoption or death. "No, I'll take him home and find his family the old-fashioned way; I'll poster every pole in Rehoboth and Lewes." It was the second time today she felt like name-calling, but she couldn't fault the vet for his reaction. What could explain her name on a strange dog's microchip?

When she got home, Gina called her on-again, off-again boyfriend. "Clark, I need you. Right now."

"Is everything okay?"

"Eddie is missing."

"Missing? How'd that happen?"

His voice sounded shocked, yet Gina detected a hint of accusation. "I don't know. It's all so weird. I need to get back to Gordons Pond to look for him."

"Get *back* to Gordons Pond? Where are you?"

"At my house."

"You left the beach without Eddie?" Definitely an accusation this time.

She couldn't waste time retelling the sequence of events. "Just get here. Please." She hung up to end the stream of questions and the implied blame.

The Lab sat on the floor next to Gina. His eyes were locked on hers as though waiting for something. Treats? That's what her Eddie always expected after their beach exercise. She took a jerky stick from the ceramic doggy jar and held it out to him. The Lab gave her his paw before taking the treat into his mouth. "Oh, my God." It was exactly what her Eddie would do. But this dog was not a golden retriever, so he couldn't be *her* Eddie. The only explanation was that whoever raised this dog had read similar dog training articles and had taught him the same etiquette.

As she watched him enjoying the dog treat, she felt sorrow for the family who must be searching for him, but more so for her own loss. She needed to continue her search.

Why was it taking so long for Clark to arrive? Screw summer traffic!

When the Labrador finished his treat, she invited him

onto the sofa and scratched behind his ears. "I'm sorry, boy. This must be hard on you, too."

The doorbell rang and, before she could answer it, the Lab rushed toward the door. "Wait a minute, Clark," she called out, as she grabbed the Lab's collar.

When she opened the door, the dog pulled away and leapt up to lick Clark's face.

"All right, all right, Eddie," Clark said. He gave the sit gesture to the Lab. Then Clark leaned in and kissed Gina's cheek. "You found him. Did someone get the info from his microchip and bring him home while I—"

Gina interrupted him. "Stop kidding, Clark. This obviously isn't my dog. My Eddie is a golden retriever."

Clark laughed. "Golden? Very funny."

"Not funny at all." The anger she had suppressed today was ready to explode.

He stopped laughing but continued to look at her as though she were playing a joke on him. "Gina, I was with you when you adopted Eddie from that Labrador retriever rescue." He put his arms around her. "Honey, are you alright? You seem confused. Maybe I should drive you to the ER. With all the stress you're under, you might be having a stroke or something."

Gina pushed away from him. "I'm not having a stroke. And my Eddie is *not* a chocolate Lab."

She held open the front door for Clark to leave.

"Call me if you need me," he said.

After he left, Gina took a cell-phone photo of the Lab and uploaded it to the LostPetsDelaware Facebook page, along with where she found him and how to contact her. Then, she opened the "Eddie" photo folder, prepared to add him to the lost pets page, too. A block of small photographs filled the screen.

She suddenly felt light-headed. The photos on her phone were pictures of a chocolate Labrador retriever—sitting by her side, walking next to her, waiting for a treat, posing in front of the fireplace in her townhouse.

That night, Gina couldn't sleep. She tossed and turned. *Why is this happening to me?* Of course, Clark was at least partially right. The transition from a regional retail store to an acquisition by a national brand had taken its toll on her.

Giving up on rest, she turned on the lights and opened her computer to compose the reviews and evaluations that were due to Barlow before the ten o'clock deadline. She couldn't save every employee or every store, but she could at least be more evenhanded than her new boss. She considered that she owed protection to the employees with the most seniority, so she typed their names under the guise of identifying them as the top salespeople who should be kept employed in the regional stores even if it meant reassigning them to stores that would remain open.

She had been so engrossed in completing the report for her new boss that she didn't notice the Lab had come into her room. She felt a lick on her ankle and reached down to pat his neck. "Tomorrow, you and I will walk every inch of the park to try to find your family. And if we don't have any luck, I'll keep you—but, you know, I'll need to change your name in case my Eddie finds his way back home." She attached her report to an email and hit send. It immediately came back as a non-existent address.

Impossible.

She examined what she had typed. The user name was correct, but a quick visit to their website should clarify whether they were a .com or a .net.

She googled "American Beauty Swimwear."

Nothing. According to her web browser, no such company existed.

Maybe she was losing her mind. It seemed the only answer.

The next morning, Clark showed up at her door. And, once again, he received an excited greeting from the Lab. While scratching under Eddie's chin, he studied Gina's face. "How are you feeling today?"

"I've been better." She pushed her hair away from her face. "I didn't sleep well, as you can see."

The Lab barked and rushed to the back door where he pawed the bell that hung there on a long ribbon. It was the signal for wanting to go outside. Once again, Gina's doubts about reality crept into her mind. She had taught her own dog, her golden, to use this method when needing to go into the fenced-in yard to do his "business."

Another coincidence? Or more than that? After she let the dog out, she said, "Clark, I'm going to ask you a strange question, but please go along with me."

"Okay." His voice indicated reluctance.

"Where do I work?"

Worry lines crossed his forehead. "Why are you asking me this?"

"Just answer me, Clark."

He crossed his arms. "Delmarva Swimsuits."

"No. I mean the new company—the one taking over."

"What new company?"

It was a *Twilight Zone* moment. Her world had somehow turned upside down. She needed time to mull this over, but more so, she needed time to talk this through. "How about having coffee with me?"

"Are you sure you're okay, Gina?"

"Of course." She filled two cups and took them to the sofa where Clark had taken a seat. "If I tell you that Delmarva Swimsuits was bought out by a large corporation, would you believe me?"

"Sure. If anyone would know about an acquisition, it would be you as the regional manager. But it can't be true or it would have been all over the local news."

"It was." She hesitated but continued. "At least, it was, according to my memory. Just as I remember a golden retriever named Eddie and a Florida-based company named American Beauty Swimwear. A dream? No. My memories are too sharp for this to be a dream. But other than my being crazy, what else could be the cause of the disparity between how *I* see the world and how *you* see it?"

Clark was quiet. He appeared to be in deep thought.

Gina sipped her coffee and waited. She hoped that he wasn't debating on whether to call 9-1-1.

"Parallel universe."

"What in the world does that mean?"

"Have you ever read *The Chronicles of Narnia*?" he asked. "That's a perfect example of a parallel universe. The kids live in England during World War II, but they step into Narnia by going inside an armoire. Both worlds live in the same space but are experienced quite differently."

Gina wished he had given her something more real as an explanation of what she was experiencing. "That's just fantasy."

"Is it? In 1957, a physicist named Hugh Everett III introduced the concept of parallel worlds. Note that he was a physicist, a scientist, not a storyteller, and not sci-fi. The belief is that we make thousands of choices throughout each day, some as simple as whether to have coffee or tea with breakfast. Every problem or decision we face has multiple ways to respond, and all the possible outcomes coexist, but in separate universes. Hence, it is possible that you and I are currently living in separate worlds." Clark held Gina's hand. "I know it *sounds* crazy, but isn't that better than *being* crazy?"

Gina looked closely at his face, trying to discern whether he was joking.

He wasn't.

"So, it's possible that I remember a golden retriever at the same time that you remember a chocolate Labrador?"

He clicked his coffee cup against hers and said in a British accent, "By Jove, I think she's got it." He gulped down the rest of his coffee. "So, now that I've solved the puzzle, I'd better get going. I don't want to be late for work at the Starbucks."

"We don't have a Starbucks here at the beach," she said.

He laughed. "Ha-ha. Very funny, Gina." He started out the door. "I'll call you after work."

She watched him walk to his car. At least the model and color were exactly right, despite all the other peculiarities she'd been experiencing over the past two days.

Gina thought about his hypothesis. *When did I step into a parallel anything?* She replayed the morning when her Eddie disappeared. Tossing the ball, answering the cell phone, then what? Yoga. The tree pose. She unrolled her yoga mat, assumed the pose, and focused on a relaxing breath.

Just then, there was a bark from the back deck. The dog was ready to come back in. And Gina was ready to accept the possibility that this chocolate Lab was her Eddie.

She opened the door, and a golden retriever entered, carrying a fluorescent green ball in his mouth. "Eddie?" At the same time, she heard a ding on her computer—the email that had been declared undeliverable was sent.

Life had returned to normal. Or had it?

What if Clark was right? What if, for a short time, two distinctly different worlds had hung in the balance: A world where Eddie was a golden retriever and Carlton Barlow of American Beauty Swimwear closed eight local stores, versus a world where a Labrador retriever had always been her Eddie and Delmarva Swimsuits continued as healthy and profitable under the leadership of sweet old Harry Chambers?

Despite her joy at the return to normalcy, she wished the latter had continued to exist in her world—she'd gladly accept Eddie as a chocolate Lab if only that meant all her colleagues at Delmarva Swimsuits still had jobs.

If only.

The Cost of Happiness

When my sister Vivian invited me to spend spring break with her in Rehoboth Beach, Delaware, as her treat, I should have known she was buttering me up for something. But the idea of staying in an ocean-view suite at the Board-walk Plaza Hotel was so tempting I didn't dare question the invitation.

On our first day there, while sipping tea and munching scones delivered from Victoria's Restaurant to our balcony at the hotel, Vivian gestured toward the ocean with a wide sweep as though she were one of those models on *The Price Is Right*. "Just look at that view, Gabby. Wouldn't you love to be able to see that the entire summer?"

"Of course, but we can't afford a summer rental."

"Who said *rental*? I'm talking about *owning* a beach house."

"Vivian, have you lost your mind? Our salaries as pub-lic-school teachers aren't enough to support homes in Bal-timore *and* Rehoboth Beach. That would mean two sets of bills—mortgage, electricity, water, Internet—due every month, whether we use the beach house or not."

"We could pool the inheritances we got from Grand-mom and put that down to reduce the monthly mortgage payment." Vivian gave me the *teacher look*, as though that would work on another teacher. "Just think of spending our summer breaks here, at less cost than two weeks in a hotel or rental. And when we retire, we'll sell our townhouses in Baltimore, move here full time, and have one set of bills split between us. We'd have extra money to spend on fun things or to put in the bank for a rainy day. But we really should act now. We'd have the mortgage paid off before we retire, and then you and I can enjoy our senior years near the ocean."

"What if one of us gets married, then what?"

"We'll cross that bridge when we get to it. And, who knows, maybe you and I will meet our future husbands here at the beach." She handed me the last scone, so I knew something big was about to be added to the discussion. "We're scheduled to tour houses for sale. The real estate agent will be arriving within the hour."

This was the kind of set-up Vivian was famous for. At least I no longer needed to wonder why she had arranged this spring vacation. "Okay. I'll look at houses with you. But I'll bet you dinner that the real estate agent won't find the house you want with a price tag we can afford."

At eleven a.m., a petite, blonde twenty-something, wearing black cropped pants with fashionable black heels and a lavender jacket over a white linen blouse, arrived at the hotel. She bubbled over with cheerleader energy. "Good morning, ladies. I'm Wendy." With a wink and grin, she flicked her pen like a magic wand. "Like in *Peter Pan*."

It took all my willpower not to roll my eyes.

She handed us her business card. Sure enough, the card identified her as Wendy. No last name, but a beach scene in the background and "Beachview Real Estate," with five contact numbers embossed in glowing gold ink.

"Before we go on our excursion, I have a gift for you." She reached into her Vera Bradley tote and removed a shiny, marine-blue folder with our names printed on the cover. "Here are the houses we'll tour today. I limited it to ten so we can fit in a light lunch. My treat, of course."

Vivian opened the folder and held it so we could both see the contents.

The first item, which was the real estate agent's headshot and resume, immediately alarmed me. "Wendy, I notice that your last name is omitted on the resume."

She smiled as though I had complimented her. "Yes, as this is a beach community, we at Beachview Real Estate prefer to take a casual and friendly approach to working with our clients. If we'd met on the beach, I would have introduced myself as Wendy; we'd never use our last names, right?"

This was an unacceptable explanation. "But we're not on the beach, and this is not a chance meeting."

Vivian jumped in, taking this stranger's side rather than mine. "I think that's great, Wendy." She removed glossy flyers containing photos and data about each of the houses and spread them across one of the beds. "Beautiful!"

While my sister arranged the brochures into a sequence of preference, Wendy handed me a page of information that Vivian must have given her in a phone conversation. "Our best ten matches to your list of must-haves."

I tried not to drop my jaw. There was no way that this co-purchase of a beach house would work out. The list proved it. My sister and I never had the same tastes. According to her selections and the house photographs strewn across the bed, Vivian dreamed of a pastel-shingled house that sits directly on the beach or overlooks the canal. She wanted cathedral ceilings and walls full of windows. Her "must-have" list included two master suites, one for each of us; this was one item we could agree on, since we had shared enough all those years we lived with our parents. Of course, in her opinion, we would also need two or three guest rooms, for all the family and friends she envisioned coming down to the beach for a visit.

"We'll start south in Fenwick Island and Bethany Beach, where there are three houses that fit your must-haves perfectly."

Vivian took an extra-large canvas tote from her suitcase and reached for the brochures.

Wendy nodded toward the papers on the bed. "You can leave those here. I have an extra folder designed specifically for the house tours, with pages for taking any notes you have during the tours." She removed a three-ring binder from her bag and held it out to Vivian.

My sister then slid the binder inside her tote, next to what looked like a scrapbook. I wondered if this was another surprise Vivian had planned.

"Shall we get started?"

My sister chose the passenger seat, as usual, relegating me to the back seat like when we were kids. This time, I was satisfied with the arrangement because, with Wendy and Vivian chatting away in the front seat, I could take some time to grasp my sister's idea of buying a second home.

As the car pulled from the parking lot, my sister passed me the scrapbook, on which she had written "Two Sisters' Beach House."

"For you, Gabby. And, before you criticize the title, it's only temporary, until you and I can agree on a name for our beach house."

"A name for our house?"

Wendy looked at me through the rearview mirror. "Naming a beach house is an old custom that's trending again."

The pages of the scrapbook were filled with magazine clippings. Most of them were photographs from *Coastal Living* magazine, while others were taken from catalogs of trendy beach furniture. She seemed to have chosen furnishings for every room of the dream house. But she crossed the line when she included her vision for *my* bedroom.

Yeah, whether Vivian had intended or not, she had successfully pushed me down memory lane to not-so-great memories of the dollhouse we shared when we were kids. Vivian took over furnishing it while I sat on my side of our bedroom and watched. The dollhouse had details that only a home decorator could provide. Vivian would walk into Clemmon's Paint Store and guilt the manager into giving her sheets of wallpaper samples to glue to the inside walls of the dollhouse. Then, she'd scour the scraps bin at JoAnn's Fabrics for prints she could turn into curtains or use to cover the plastic dollhouse furniture. You'd think that, when she grew up, she'd have gotten a degree in interior design, but she became a math teacher instead. Go figure. Maybe it was all the calculations she did when dressing the dollhouse. While Mom thought we were playing together, I was lying on my bed reading books or making up stories in my mind about the residents of the dollhouse. Hence, my college degree in English Lit.

The house in Fenwick Island was a massive oceanfront house, raised atop thick wood pilings. Wendy parked on a car pad under the house, and Vivian and I discovered that the ground-level entrance had an elevator, which delivered us to the first floor.

"This is the sleeping and bath level of the home," said Wendy, as we walked into a large sitting room with hallways jutting off in three directions. "Technically, there is only one master bedroom suite; however, there is a second bedroom, with an en-suite bathroom. Although that one has a slightly smaller walk-in closet."

My room, of course. But I was less concerned with the size of my potential bedroom than I was of the layout of the house. "Why is the sleeping and bath area on the first floor?"

Wendy's eyes widened and she smiled, but she couldn't hide the slightly condescending tone of her voice. "It's logical. Why waste the best views on a floor where you spend hours asleep? The living areas are often at the top of beachfronts, so you can see the ocean during your waking hours."

I grinned at my sister. "Hey, Viv, maybe we could call it 'Upside-Down Beach House.'"

Vivian was not amused. "Wendy is right, Gabby. Whenever I've watched *Buying the Beach* and *Beachfront Bargain Hunt* on TV, I've noticed that on-the-beach houses do tend to be arranged that way."

I mimicked Wendy's smile and, in my most sarcastic

tone, said to my sister, "Well, maybe if I had known we'd be shopping for a beach house, I might have done a bit of research, too."

The third floor and rooftop deck were impressive. The living room was open concept, with a mammoth gas fireplace surrounded by floor-to-ceiling stonework. The furniture and décor were high-end, yet beachy. The kitchen held top-of-the-line stainless steel appliances and a marble island with teak barstools. But the pièce de résistance was the rooftop deck with two immense pergolas wrapped in strings of white lights, one covering a Jacuzzi and the other providing shade to the cushioned chaise lounges, an oversized teak table that could seat fourteen people, and a brick barbeque island complete with gas grill and food prep spaces.

Certainly, the house was beautiful, but I was fairly sure there was no way my sister and I could afford it, not even with our inheritance from Granny. "So, what's something like this cost?"

Wendy winked. "It's priced to move at two-and-a-half million."

The price tag made even my sister inhale so deeply that her voice jumped an octave. "Two-and-a-half-million dollars?"

"And change," Wendy added. "It's an absolute steal considering the view, the amount of property, and the high-end materials used. Imported Italian marble throughout the house, hand-scarped wide-plank floors, built-in technology like full-house surround sound. And keep in mind that Jacuzzi on the rooftop deck."

I watched my sister's face drop. "Do you have any listings that are less?" she asked the agent.

Wendy lips tightened but she forced a smile. "Not if you want a single-family oceanfront home." She flipped through her folder and didn't look up. "Anything that close to the beach will be at least a million, even for a fixer-upper. Townhouses here go for upwards of one-and-a-half-million dollars when they're oceanfront like this house. If you had shared your financial status, I would have informed you that *oceanfront* and *your specifications* were incompatible with your bottom line." She closed the book, sighed, and suggested that we consider a condominium. "Of course, an ocean-view unit will be close to a million unless you're satisfied with a small, two-bedroom, one-bath, cramped unit, with either limited or no view of the ocean."

Vivian was quiet and reserved as we toured several condominiums in the Bethany Beach area. But no problem: Wendy talked nonstop about the joys of living at the beach. "The ocean view from the condos in this building is spectacular. And the amenities—"

My sister cut her off. "The amenities don't make up for the feeling of living in a cubicle. There's no beach house feeling here."

"Of course, when you add your own touches, any residence can be as beachy as you'd like." Wendy surely noticed that my sister was about to explode. She suggested a quick lunch at Mango's. "It's right on the boardwalk, so we can enjoy watching the ocean while we eat."

Lunch was delicious, though I doubted Vivian was enjoying the taste of her meal. She stabbed the shrimp in her Caesar salad, stared at it while swirling it in the dressing, as though in a trance, before she lifted it to her mouth and chewed so slowly that I wondered if she were stalling the act of touring more condos afterward.

As any good sister would, I covered for her by participating in mind-numbing conversation with Wendy, who, though she never gave her last name, gleefully supplied her whole life story. She was a child model, whose business-empire family traveled around the world until finally settling in coastal Delaware. An athlete and lifeguard during high school, she became a licensed real estate agent with plans to eventually own her own company and was engaged to the "most handsome and talented man in Lewes." I imagined his biggest talent was listening to her—if he actually existed. I had my doubts. Whenever I asked her for specifics about her wondrous life experiences, she only shared irrelevant details.

By now, I was concerned that this young woman was more of a con artist than a real estate agent. Vivian had better insist we visit the brick-and-mortar office of Beachview Real Estate and see proof of Wendy's credentials before any contract was signed.

After lunch, Vivian complained, "Other than the mansion we can't afford, what you've shown us has nothing to do with any of my must-haves. It's like you're showing us junk so you can wear us down to the point where we might purchase what will get you the biggest commission."

"Viv," I said, hoping to alert her to how nasty that sounded. Despite my own misgivings about the agent's qualifications and motivation, I thought we at least owed polite behavior toward Wendy for the lunch she had provided.

It worked. My sister lightened her tone. "I'm sorry, Wendy. I didn't mean that the way it sounded. It's this headache

I have. It's making me grouchy. Could we call it a day, and pick up the rest of the showings later this week?"

Apparently, this wasn't the first time Wendy had encountered sticker shock in a new client. "I wish you'd been upfront about your budget. Perhaps you two could compare notes about the places you've seen today—what you liked, what you didn't like, and a realistic price point. Text me, and I assure you that I can find the perfect summer home to satisfy both of you."

Back in our room at the Boardwalk Plaza, Vivian gathered the real estate papers from her bed and deposited them in messy pile on the bureau. She stared at the top paper and seemed deep in thought.

"Viv, are you okay?"

When she held up the paper, I saw that it was the agent's headshot and resume. "Did you buy her explanation for why she goes by just her first name? Beach casual? Really?"

"I did think it suspect. Maybe we should call the main office of *Beachview Real Estate* before we make any commitment to a purchase."

"Agreed." Vivian dropped the resume on the bureau. "Well, one good thing came out of today's mess—You get to collect on the dinner I owe you. You won the bet. What was I thinking when I imagined us living in an oceanfront *House Beautiful*?"

During a sushi dinner on the outside deck of The Cultured Pearl, we talked about everything except moving to coastal Delaware, with both of us trying to ignore the underlying tension that hung in the air. But when the banana tempura and Irish coffees arrived, Vivian addressed the issue. "As far as I'm concerned, Gabby, we can stop the search. You were right. We can't afford a beach house."

"Sure, we can." I couldn't believe I was saying this, but I could see my sister's eyes tearing up. "We just can't afford one of *those* beach houses. So, we have to change our idea of a beach house."

Vivian pushed a chunk of fried banana around in the chocolate syrup. "It isn't a beach house if it isn't on the water. Being able to see the ocean is the whole point."

"Viv, stand up and look to your left. There it is—the ocean! Even though it's three blocks from the beach, it's still an ocean view. So why not at least check if there are any houses on the side streets in Rehoboth or other areas that might be more affordable?" Then, I couldn't help teasing her. "And we could name it 'Almost a Beach View House.'"

Maybe it was the sugar high from the dessert or the whiskey in the coffee, but Vivian pulled out her cell phone and started typing. "I'll text Wendy No-Name about our decision to widen the search."

The next morning, Wendy, again dressed in fashionable professional clothing with sandals and a cute sunhat to add the beach element, was still energetic and positive, though it seemed a bit more forced. She insisted on driving us up and down the side streets of Rehoboth rather than having us walk—perhaps she was afraid we'd become too aware of how far we were from the ocean, a reason not to buy.

Houses anywhere near the beach were still too expensive, and any that were under a million dollars would be money pits for the repairs needed. After walking through what seemed to have been the home of a hoarder, Vivian announced, "I'm done."

Wendy seemed irritated and relieved at the same time. "You have my contact information should you decide to take a second look at any of the homes I showed you."

We both thanked her with the same forced pleasantry she had given us throughout the day. And when we stepped out of her car at the entrance to the hotel, the agent click-locked the car doors and sped away.

If it's possible to wave sarcastically, then that's exactly how my sister Vivian waved at Wendy. "Well, that says it all. If, and I do mean if, I ever decide to pick up my search for a beach house, it won't be with Ms. No-Name." She dropped the Beachview Real Estate folder into the nearest garbage can. "I guess we should have dunch, my treat."

"Dunch?" I asked.

Vivian grinned. "Dinner and lunch combined. How about the outside tables at Victoria's?"

With the beach house plans dropped, I could finally relax and enjoy time with my sister. As we sipped char-donnay and shared baked brie, the words *house*, *cottage*, *beachfront*, and *ocean view* were replaced with *remember when*, *outlet shopping*, and *beach umbrellas*. Dinner was followed by a boardwalk stroll to work off the calories and the alcohol. This was exactly the type of beach visit I'd choose for spending time with my sister.

The stress had taken a toll on Vivian. She woke up with a migraine, or maybe a hangover, but in either case, she was determined to spend the day with the Hallmark channel and room service. Though I sometimes partook of that kind of relaxation myself, I refused to stay indoors on such a beautiful sunny day. "Come on, Viv, let's get you some strong espresso and a couple of Excedrin to clear up your headache. It would be a shame to throw away a vacation day."

"It's not a throw away. It's self-indulgent. Think of it as a spa day. China tea cups with imported tea and freshly baked scones with just the push of a telephone button."

"I spent two days with you and a Barbie-doll real estate agent touring houses I don't want. You owe me! Just for today, go along with *my* plans. You know that Lori, the sophomore counselor at school, has a place nearby, right? She told me she'll be spending her vacation there. Why don't we catch up with her?"

"I heard she has a trailer, not a house."

"Knock it off, Miss Snippy. I never said she has a *house*. I said she has a *place*. By the way, it's called a mobile home, not a trailer. It would be nice to visit her."

"Maybe later in the week. I need a day to recover." Vivian stacked her pillows and reached for the remote control. "But you don't have to stick around. Take my car keys and go visit Lori." She pointed to her purse on the table, and I tossed it to her, trying not to aim at her head, though the thought had crossed my mind.

"And when she asks where you are?"

"Tell her about our horrific two days of house hunting and she'll believe it when you say I have a headache." She handed me the keys.

As I walked toward the door, Vivian called out, "Take pictures for me, okay? I don't want to hurt Lori's feelings."

Lori's mobile home was part of a community called Aspen Meadows, on a quiet back street, close to Route 1 yet secluded enough to be clear of the noise of that busy highway. When I pulled into the community, I was surprised by how different it was from what I had imagined. Aspen Meadows was surrounded by lush trees and shrubs, and the mobile homes seemed more like one-story cottages. There were porches, gardens, and landscaped lawns. As I turned onto Buttermilk Drive, I saw Lori standing on a redwood deck and waving me onto the parking pad in front of her home.

When I joined her on the deck, Lori handed me a glass of white wine. "Welcome to my beach house. Where's Vivian?"

"Nursing a migraine back at the hotel."

"Too bad. My husband and kids are at a Boy Scout campout in Cape Henlopen State Park tonight, so momma's free to party. Drinks are here on the deck, hamburgers on the grill and then outlet shopping. If we're not exhausted after that, we can get iced coffee at Browseabout Books and go for a walk on the boardwalk."

I clicked wine glasses with Lori. "Where do we begin?"

She pointed to her front door. "How about a tour?"

"Perfect. Vivian told me to take pictures." I opened my cell phone and clicked a few photographs of the front of the house, French entrance doors with sectioned glass insets, the natural wood Adirondack chairs in front of the wide windows, the multi-level flower beds that edged the deck. "This is a mobile? I can't believe it."

Lori nodded. "Yeah. If I say that I have a beach house, everyone at school pictures one of those luxurious mansions along the ocean. But if I say it's a mobile, everyone thinks I have a camper on a plot of backcountry land." She showed me a hand-painted sign hanging on the railing of the deck. "'Bored of Education.' Get it? That's what we call our mobile."

"So, Vivian and the real estate agent were right about the trendiness of house naming. Wow."

Following my sister's request, I took photos of each room. The front third of the mobile, or what Lori called a double-wide, was open-space concept—a huge area with a combination living room/dining room section and a kitchen with counter seating separating it from the other parts. Down the hallway, there was a spacious master bedroom with an en-suite bathroom that even Vivian would like. The other two bedrooms, which shared a full bath, provided a bedroom for Lori's two boys and an additional guest bedroom. There was even a laundry room with a washer, dryer, and storage. This was more space than I had in my townhouse in Baltimore. "I want one of these."

"If you mean it, there's a great double-wide like this for sale just down the street. It's even better than ours. The two guys who own it totally redid the inside. It's like something out of *Architectural Digest*. It has two master suites. I'd buy it, but we're already attached to this one." A wicked grin crossed Lori's face, and she put down her wine glass. "Let's go look at it."

"I don't think I have the energy to see one more house."

"But, Gabby, M2 won't stay on the market for long."

"M2? What?"

Lori laughed. "Maison de Martini, or M2 for short. That's the name Randall and Sean gave their mobile. The guys are known for their martini soirees. I'm telling you, Gabby, you need to see this place. It's better than some of the small cottages downtown. And it's such a good deal, considering the work the guys put into it. You owe it to yourself to check it out before it gets snapped up. Besides, I want an excuse to see it one more time before new owners move in."

As we arrived at Maison de Martini, a real estate agent was shaking hands with a client. Lori whispered, "Damn! I bet we're too late."

But as the guy got into his car, the agent approached us with her business card. "Good morning, ladies. I'm the listing agent, Judith Henson of Coastal Mobile Realty."

A real estate agent with a last name.

"Are we too late to check out this mobile?" Lori asked.

"No. Offers are still being accepted." And with that, she showed us Maison de Martini.

Everything Lori had said about it was true. A wrap-around deck, an enclosed garden area with a firepit, and a storage shed that had been redesigned into a screened seating area with a wet bar, fridge, and microwave. The interior looked like a spread in a magazine—a cross between Manhattan cool and summer casual. I fell in love immediately. "How much are the owners asking?"

"The list price is $130,000, but there is already an offer of $139,000."

After the price tags on the mini-mansions and the cubicle-sized condos, the price seemed a bargain. I could probably even buy it without Vivian's money if she decided that Maison de Martini was not to her liking. It was certainly to my liking.

"Would you like to make an offer?" Judith asked. "All you need to do is put down a good-faith deposit to start the bidding. Then, if you decide to not go through with the purchase, your deposit will be returned in full."

Lori played cheerleader in the background. "Come on, Gabby! My place is just down the street from here; we'd be neighbors. Think of the benefits. You get built-in friends who will keep an eye on your house when you can't be here."

"How much does the good-faith deposit need to be?"

"How about $500?" the agent suggested.

I should have said no. I should have considered my sister's dream of a house with a water view. I should have at least called Vivian before I took out my credit card. But I didn't. "I'll offer $139,500."

Lori couldn't hide her enthusiasm. "For gosh sakes, take photographs to show Vivian. She'll fall in love with this place!"

While the agent set up paperwork, I clicked away, though I wondered how I was going to break the news to my sister. If I bought this mobile, then she couldn't depend on me to split the cost of a beach house with her. Of course, she could share this one with me, but without a view of any body of water other than the community swimming pool, I knew she would not be enthusiastic about joint ownership, especially of a *trailer* (as she would call it).

As the sales agent locked M2, I got worried and considered withdrawing my bid. "What did I just do?"

"You just bid on a beach house," Lori said. "This is exciting! Let's skip the cookout and go to the hotel to tell your sister and show her the photographs."

"No!"

"Why not? You told me the search for her kind of beach house was a disaster. M2 is the clear answer. With the two of you splitting the cost and the bills … Oh, I see what you mean." Lori knew my sister well enough. "The beach house was Vivian's idea, but you beat her to it. Yeah, she'll be pissed, won't she?"

"This will certainly give her a bigger headache than she has right now, so I'm not going to mention it yet. I'll wait for a week or two before I break the news. Besides, I might not have bid enough to get the mobile anyway, so why get Vivian upset for something that isn't a sure thing."

The plan worked—at least for a while. The next day, when Lori drove to the hotel and joined my sister and me for brunch, nothing was mentioned about M2, even though Vivian recounted her stories about the two days of house hunting with Wendy No-Name.

Lori said, "That's why my husband and I bought a mobile. Way less money, yet plenty of room for us and the boys."

Vivian's face looked doubtful, as she undoubtedly pictured a skinny house on wheels. "Gabby, you haven't shown me photos of the mobile. Did you remember to take some?"

At first, I thought she was talking about Maison de Martini, but how would she know about that? Thankfully, I realized she meant photographs of Lori's mobile. "Of course, I took photos." I opened my cell phone app and clicked each photo individually as I described the areas. The final photo was of the landscaping in front of Lori's home. "And your favorite tree—crepe myrtle."

Vivian grabbed my phone to get a closer look at the pink crepe myrtle. "Beautiful." Then, before I could retrieve my phone, she slid her finger across the screen to look at the next photo. "Maison de Martini? What's this?"

I answered before Lori could slip up. "It's a mobile Lori showed me in her neighborhood." I held out my hand, but Vivian kept flipping through the photographs.

"You went inside and took photos?"

Lori had a panicked look on her face. "Yeah. It belongs to friends of mine. I wanted Gabby to see how talented they are at interior design."

Vivian nodded. She expanded one of the photos, but I couldn't see which one. Then she clicked around, and I got the feeling she sent a copy of one of the photographs to someone, probably herself, though I don't know why she would do that. In any case, she finally handed me my cell phone. I was uncertain whether I had dodged the bullet, but nothing more was said about M2.

The day was getting more and more overcast, so Lori suggested we return to the outlets.

Vivian poured herself another cup of tea. "Why don't you and Gabby go without me? I'm not interested in buying clothes until I drop a few more pounds."

"We could do something else. Go to a movie? The outlets were just an idea," Lori said.

"Thanks, but I feel like being on my own for the day."

"Again?" Lori and I both said at the same time.

"Your birthday is in three weeks, Gabby. I plan to shop in Lewes for your present. Now do you understand why I want to be alone today?"

Lori and I were in our third store when my phone rang. It was Judith, the real estate agent for Maison de Martini. "I'm afraid you've been outbid."

When she asked me if I wanted to counter, my mouth said, "Yes. $139, 650." After I hung up, my brain said, *Are you nuts? You're scared to tell your sister about the first bid, and now you've made a second one.*

A few stores later, another phone call with another counterbid. Again, I raised mine. "$139,725."

During a coffee break at Starbucks, another step in the bidding war. "$139,850."

Lori said, "Gabby, are you sure? M2 is gorgeous, but you still haven't told your sister about it. Don't you think you should say something to her before you go any farther?"

She was right, of course. "Let's go by Maison de Martini so I can get one more look at it to be sure it's what I want. I certainly don't want to get into a disagreement with my sister about buying a mobile unless I'm sure that I love the place and not just the excitement of bidding."

We tossed our shopping bags into Lori's car and headed toward Aspen Meadows. As we pulled up to M2, I saw a familiar car parked there. "Lori, that's Vivian's car. Quick, drive away. Take me to your house."

I phoned my sister. "Viv, how's your day going?"

"Wonderfully. How's yours?"

"Good. Lori and I are taking a break from shopping. I'm at her house."

"Well, have fun. Look, I've gotta go, Gabby. I don't like to talk on the phone while walking. I don't want to be one of those people who falls over a wall or something and ends up on a Facebook video."

As soon as I clicked off, I checked the Find My Friends app. Sure enough, Vivian was still at Maison de Martini. "Hah!" But before I could share my findings with Lori, my phone rang. This time, it wasn't my sister. It was Judith. "We have another bid. $140,000. Do you want to counter?"

"No. I withdraw my bid. Please credit $500 back to my card."

Lori's jaw dropped. "What did you just do? You were so close to getting M2."

I smiled. "I think I found a way to have my mobile and still keep my sister happy. But it's going to take a solemn promise from you that you'll never tell Vivian I bid on M2."

Lori broke out into a loud laugh. "So, you think Vivian's the other bidder?"

"Yep. I think my sister was impressed by the photos and devised her own plan to check out the place. I don't know how she found M2 or the agent, but …" I opened my photo app and looked over the pictures of Maison de Martini until I found my answer. "The sign in the front window! It has the agent's name and phone number. And the address of the mobile is on the mailbox."

"This is exhausting. Let me fix us something to drink.

Hey, how about a mango smoothie?"

Just as I finished my first smoothie and was getting ready to start a second one, Vivian drove up to Lori's house. "Surprise! I've come to visit."

I handed her my smoothie. "How'd you find Lori's house?"

"Find My Friends. What a great app!" (If only she knew.) "I'm glad you talked me into downloading it." Vivian reached into her purse and took out a folded packet of paper. "Gabby, I've got exciting news for you. That mobile you took pictures of yesterday—I visited it today. And I bought it. We have a beach house! Isn't that great?"

I pretended to be shocked, but I didn't need to pretend my excitement. "That's wonderful!

She handed the paper and a pen to me. "You just need to sign on the line and we're co-owners of a classy double-wide in Aspen Meadows."

As I wrote my name, I said, "And this one we can really call 'Two Sisters' Beach House.'"

Mayonnaise Jars and a Yellow Quilt

Seeing the "For Sale" sign for the first time took Kendra's breath away. It was all real now—the loss of the beach house and her fear that her marriage to Bryan was crumbling. Four weeks ago, he delegated the task of clearing out the cottage to her. "After all, the semester's over by then, and you'll be on summer break. I'll be stuck in the stacks at McKeldin working on my dissertation."

Stuck in the stacks? She might have laughed at the alliteration if she hadn't been so upset. She would have given anything to be in graduate school, but when they couldn't afford to be minus two salaries, she had agreed to keep teaching while he went back to college. Already, that decision had taken its toll. Her salary was not enough to keep two houses going—their real house in Towson, Maryland, and their vacation home here in Fenwick Island, Delaware. She noted the difference in how she identified one as a house and the other as a home. Of the two, she would rather give up their Maryland house, but that would be ridiculous since they both were teachers in Maryland. Well, at least, she was a teacher there; Bryan hadn't taught in two years, as he had taken a leave of absence to focus on graduate school.

"So, how am I to decide what to keep and what to toss?" she had asked.

"I don't have time for this, Kendra," he snapped back.

"Toss anything or everything." Rhyming, this time. Probably the effect of his graduate studies in linguistics. Linguistics? Why? How would that specialty help them stay afloat when it was her turn to go to grad school?

She strode to the door and jammed the key into the lock. But it wouldn't turn. She tried again and again, each time with more force. Still, no success. "Damn, damn, damn!" Each "damn" was more emphatic.

"Having fun?"

Her heart jumped. She didn't immediately recognize the voice, but when she turned around, she was relieved to see that it was one of their summer neighbors, standing at the end of the driveway. "The stupid key won't turn."

"Humidity's kinda high today. Try pulling the door toward you."

She pulled. The key turned. "Thanks."

"Bryan coming later?"

She hoped her smile was believable. "No. Only me."

"I see you're selling the place."

A quick nod, then she leaned her shoulder against the door and pushed into the house, taking an extra moment to give a tiny thank-you wave before dropping her weekender and purse on the hall bench.

The house was stuffy from being closed all winter and spring. A wave of nausea came over her. She walked into the family room, opened the side panels of the bay window, and sat on the window seat to breathe in the fresh air of early summer. The steady breeze lifted the faded blue dotted swiss curtains and sent them dancing in its flow. She'd made the curtains eight summers ago, the summer she and Bryan had bought this place. Her fingers ached at the memory of that long day of measuring the three angled windows, drafting the pattern, pinning and cutting and stitching the light fabric, determined to hang the finished curtains in the window by evening. Bryan had kissed her neck when she lifted the curtain rod into place. He had told her how pretty the curtains were. "But not as pretty as my beautiful wife."

Whatever.

The musty smell of the cottage dispersed, but Kendra's stomach refused to settle down. She reached for her purse, for the Tums Antacid Smoothies she'd been popping like candy the last few weeks. She shook four tablets into her hand and crunched them one by one in her mouth. With school over, she had to admit that it wasn't her students causing her stomach issues. It was her dread of selling the beach home.

Suddenly, the reality of her situation—depleted savings combined with credit-card debt—made her see the cottage through eyes of mourning. She was saying goodbye to the happy place where she and Bryan had spent relaxing days and romantic evenings.

She put her feet up on the window seat, wrapped her arms around her knees in a hug of comfort, and studied the room as though it were a museum display. An open-space first floor, divided by a wide kitchen island with stools on both sides. The furniture, shabby chic before it became the predominant style of makeover TV shows. The overstuffed sofa where Bryan would nap in the afternoon, covered by the yellow quilt his mother bought them during a shopping trip to the quaint little town of Berlin, Maryland. The fire-place mantel with five-inch whitewashed wooden blocks that spelled *F A M I L Y* in multi-colored alphabet letters.

She had bought the blocks at the Seaside Country Store three summers ago when she thought she might be pregnant. She wasn't. The doctor blamed the false alarm on stress and wishful thinking. She and Bryan had been trying too hard to have a child. The doctor's advice: "Give it time." They had. Lots of time. Too much time. Time enough for Bryan to apply to the doctorate program at University of Maryland, College Park, get accepted, and be approved for a two-year leave of absence from his job as a high school English teacher. Time enough for Kendra to feel their marriage slipping away like the tide.

A few months ago, she'd walked into the bonus room of their Towson townhouse, where her husband was typing an outline for his doctoral dissertation. She had stood at the doorway and watched as his fingers flew over the keyboard and imagined them caressing her.

"What do you want, Kendra?" He hadn't looked up from the computer.

She'd answered, "Nothing," and walked away. She hadn't expected him to follow her.

Inside their bedroom, she'd laid on the bed, staring straight ahead at the wall of photographs. Skiing at Killington. Toasting marshmallows over a firepit in Fenwick Island. Their formal wedding portrait and, tucked into the lower corner of the frame, a goofy wedding snapshot taken by one of their friends. That was her favorite. It captured who they really were. Spontaneous. Fun. Social. *Were*. Past tense.

When she'd heard the computer shut down, she figured that Bryan would make his way to the kitchen and stand at the refrigerator, grazing on unheated leftovers. Instead, he came into the bedroom and lay beside her. For a moment, they were both looking at the photos. She wondered what he was thinking and whether he would tell her. She doubted that he'd apologize. "You could have been a fashion model," he said. Then he rolled onto his side and kissed her. It wasn't an apology of words, but it felt like an apology anyway. She returned his kiss, and within minutes, they were wrapped together in a way that physical communication existed where spoken thoughts could not. The next morning, neither of them mentioned their lovemaking. She told herself not to expect intimacy in the future; that night was an anomaly.

She was right. A week later, Bryan stopped coming home, though he did leave a note for her on the coffee table.

Kendra, I think it's best that I stay with my brother Jake. His condo is walking distance from the university. It will save us money in gas, tolls, and wear and tear on my car. It will also give me easy access to the university library and, since Jake is seldom home, it will make the dissertation easier to write. Love, Bryan.

She filled in what was unsaid: She was an unwelcome distraction. And he no longer needed her by his side.

She wondered how the living arrangement was working out. Her brother-in-law was a player. Bars. Parties. King of the one-night-stands. Jake was a fun guy to have around, but she didn't trust him. She worried that her husband would be so overwhelmed by the stress of graduate work that he'd get caught up in his brother's lifestyle.

A stronger wave of nausea washed over her, and she ran to the kitchen, hoping to find some crackers or cereal. There was half sleeve of saltines, a bit stale but helpful. She sat on one of the stools and crunched the crackers slowly, letting the salty taste linger on her tongue.

What if Bryan found happiness in someone else's arms, someone who would not be demanding, whiny, or whatever adjective he'd choose to describe her? If only she had shown more interest in his doctoral studies. If only she had stopped bugging him about having a child. If only.

F A M I L Y. The word mocked her from its place on the mantel. She made a beeline to the fireplace and, with one long strike, scattered the letters across the floor. Four of them landed beside each other, like in a game of Scrabble, and spelled *F A I L.*

She sank onto the sofa and stared at the word. *Fail.* For the first eleven years of their marriage, she and Bryan were teachers, sharing a profession with highs and lows and piles of papers to grade every night, but weekends filled with social events and a great circle of friends, dancing, drinking, and cheering on the O's and the Ravens. Then it all collapsed. The other couples became parents. But she and Bryan didn't. Neither of them blamed the other, at least not aloud. Fertility doctors and fertility drugs, with high price tags and no results. Fertility schedules, resulting in scientific sex that was neither loving nor productive. Fertility failure.

Across from the sofa stood the Craftsman bookcase that she and Bryan had bought at a yard sale the first summer they stayed here. Together, they had restored it, sanding down the multiple layers of varnish and giving it a whitewash finish to complement the beach décor of their summer cottage. It was crammed with battered paperbacks, but the top shelf showcased rows of mayonnaise jars filled with shells that she and Bryan had collected together. Each year, they started the summer with a clean jar on which Kendra glued an oval of linen with the year cross-stitched in royal blue. Each jar of shells was a record of that summer.

She saw that the last two jars were only half full. Kendra had collected those shells during solo walks she made on the beach, pretending she enjoyed the solitude of the morning when, in reality, she was ever hopeful that Bryan would soon follow. He never did. She should have realized their marriage was on shaky ground. But denial is more than a river in Egypt.

She crossed to the bookshelf and, one by one, threw the jars against the hardwood floor, sending chucks of thick glass and smashed seashells in curving paths across the room. Each jar increased her fury, and each crash was stronger and scattered farther. But when she touched the final jar, the one they'd made during that first summer, a bluish-purple shell shaped like a heart stopped her hand. She reached into the jar and removed the special shell and cradled it in her palm. She felt an odd maternal affection for this oddly-shaped shell. This was the one that had started their obsession with collecting seashells. She held it in the air to let the sunshine from the bay window illuminate the faint pastel color that swirled over its surface.

Then she caught sight of the yellow quilt hanging on the back of the sofa—the quilt Bryan's mother had bought. The summer after buying them that quilt, his mother had lost her battle with colon cancer—the cancer that scared Kendra as she read the symptoms she feared might be wreaking havoc in her own body. This fear had prompted a visit to a GI specialist, a scheduled colonoscopy, and blood tests, the results of which she awaited.

She hadn't told Bryan any of this. If the words weren't

said, then she could continue to hope. Was it a mistake to keep silent? If she *had* told him about her symptoms, then maybe he would be here standing by her side right now, holding her in his arms, and waiting for the results from the doctor. But, although that would be good for her, it would be terrible for Bryan. It would bring back memories of his mother's struggle and how he watched as his mom lost her hair and skin tone, then her weight and her strength, until she could no longer fight the cancer. No.

Kendra still loved her husband enough that she couldn't put him through that. Not yet, at least. Not until she knew her own diagnosis. And only then.

Feelings of fear and abandonment swept over her. It wasn't fair that she was carrying this burden alone. Bryan should have paid attention to her—should have sensed that she was going through something. *Damn him and his grad school preoccupation.*

Kendra flung the seashell and the final jar to the floor, watching the glass bottom of the jar shatter the heart into two unequal pieces. *How fitting*, she thought. *Yet tragic.* Her anger let go into an uncontrollable wailing of words that hung in the air too long and fell into unfinished sentences. "Why did …" and "I wish that …" and "I want …" She tried to complete each thought, but every possible ending was unsuccessful and dropped off. Her mind was stuck. She wrapped up in the yellow quilt and hugged it to herself like a drowning person clutches a life preserver. "I want my life back."

She heard music coming from her purse, and it took her a moment to realize that it was her cell phone, and a moment longer to listen to the unfamiliar ringtone. Curiosity made her retrieve the phone to check the caller ID. Felicia Wilson. The real estate agent was probably calling to check on her progress.

Kendra set the phone to "Do Not Disturb" and tossed it on the sofa. "This is my house, too!" she screamed. "And maybe I'll keep it." But how could she afford to handle the bills for another year if Bryan's dissertation wasn't completed on time or if it wasn't accepted on his first try? And what if the distance between them that had developed over the past two years ended in his request for a separation?

She considered her options. Bryan could have the Towson townhouse, and she could look for a teaching job near the beach and make this cottage her full-time home. But even if she could keep this place and find a teaching position within driving distance, how could she live here alone with the ghost of their marriage walking the floors each night?

Another wave of nausea coursed through her. She hurried to the kitchen sink, where she ran a stream of icy water over her wrists until the sick feeling went away. *Maybe I'm just hungry.* Her breakfast had been only a venti latte she'd bought at the Starbucks on Route 50 on her way to Fenwick Island. And the stale saltines hadn't stopped the growling in her stomach. She needed real breakfast food—like a homemade Belgian waffle from Dirty Harry's to mend her stomach and brighten her mood. Maybe.

She grabbed her keys and purse and drove up Coastal Highway to the restaurant. On the way, she realized she had forgotten her phone, but she was too hungry to turn back now and figured she wouldn't be gone long.

She was seated immediately by an older waitress named Jean who remembered her from previous summers. "Welcome back, honey!" The waitress poured one glass of water and started to pour a second one.

Kendra placed her hand over the extra glass on the table. "No. I'm eating alone today."

"No hubby to bother you this weekend, huh? Lucky you!"

"Lucky me." Her answer was simple, short, and enough. She didn't feel the need to add details, though if she were seated at a bar and deep in booze, she might unburden her woes on a bartender. "I'd like a Belgian waffle and some tea. No, make that two Belgian waffles and …" She scanned the menu. "Scrapple, grits, and eggs over easy. With hot sauce."

"You must be starved." Then, Jean leaned over and asked softly, "Or are you and your hubby expecting?"

Kendra's face burned. "No. We can't have kids."

It was the waitress's turn to blush. "Oh. I'm so sorry." She turned and rushed into the kitchen.

Kendra wished she hadn't left her cell phone at the beach house. She could use some digital distraction and felt awkward sitting alone. She looked around the room to see if there were any other one-person tables, but saw only twos, threes, and fours, chatting and laughing while enjoying breakfast.

A young man with the shoulders of a football player, carrying a large round tray, delivered her breakfast. The food she'd ordered covered the entire table. It looked like an old-fashioned smorgasbord. She picked at each of the foods a little until she determined that the scrapple and the eggs with hot sauce were probably not good choices for an uneasy stomach. But the waffles, her reason for going to Dirty Harry's in the first place, were exactly what she needed. Delicious and comforting.

When she put down her fork and wiped her mouth with the napkin, a young girl with an eastern European accent stopped by to remove some of the dishes. "Are you finished with these?"

Kendra gave a long sigh. "Absolutely. I couldn't eat another bite. I can't believe I ordered all this."

The girl stacked the dishes. "Our eyes are always bigger than our stomachs."

Kendra looked around the restaurant. There was no sign of her original waitress. "Where's Jean?"

The girl's face showed that she was lying when she answered, "She's on break."

Kendra felt bad as she remembered the horrified look on the waitress's face on hearing her say that she couldn't have children. "Please tell Jean I'm very happy she remembered me and my husband. She made my day."

When the check for the meal was brought to the table, it was Jean who delivered it. "I'm glad that you enjoyed your breakfast." She didn't mention the message given to the younger waitress, but it was obvious to Kendra that the message had been received. "We like to take care of our regulars, you know. We think of you as our family."

As Kendra pulled out of the parking lot, she reflected on what Jean had said. There was that word "family" again. She thought of the wooden letters, now scattered around the family room. And the broken glass and shattered seashells. Nothing a good broom and dustpan couldn't clean away. She could put the letters back together on the mantel—*F A M I L Y*—but that couldn't change the hard truth that Kendra wasn't going to be a mother. And maybe wasn't going to be a wife, either. And what if she had to face cancer alone?

She thought about her profession—teaching. She started over each year with new students and, sometimes, new subjects to teach or a new curriculum to present. Despite all the unknowns, everything always fell into place. Perhaps by starting over in her personal life, things would fall into place for her, too.

Her optimism tanked when she reached the driveway to the beach house and saw a police car parked there. Panic ran up her spine. What was wrong? Why would the police be at her home? Did something happen to Bryan? Her chest tightened. *Please don't let anything be wrong with Bryan.*

She pulled the car onto the gravel and hurried into the cottage. In the family room, an officer was taking photographs of the broken glass and, surprisingly, her husband was there, seated on the sofa, his face ashen.

"Bryan, where's your car?"

He dashed across the room and held her tightly in his arms. "Kendra, you're okay? I thought something terrible had happened to you."

Wrapped in his embrace, tears rolled down her cheeks. "I'm fine, but why is there a police officer here with you?"

"My car broke down on Route 54 and had to be towed. The officer gave me a lift when I told him I was on my way to check on my wife because you weren't answering your cell phone even though the Find My Friends app indicated you were at the beach house. I was afraid that you were sick or hurt. When we got here and saw this mess and your cell phone abandoned on the sofa, he and I both thought the worst."

"This?" she asked, nodding toward the mess on the floor, not letting go of her husband. "My fault. I had a few accidents with breakables. Sorry. I'll clean it up."

The officer, realizing that this wasn't a crime scene after all, cancelled the missing person's report and left.

"Kendra, where were you?" Bryan asked.

"I got breakfast at Dirty Harry's."

"And your cell phone? You never go anywhere without your cell phone."

"I forgot it. Probably because I didn't want to talk to the real estate agent."

"Why not?"

"I want to keep this place. I'm willing to stay here year-round and find a local teaching job to pay the bills for the cottage. And since we're not much of a married couple anymore, maybe it would be better if you're free to go wherever your PhD might lead you. We can always sell the townhouse."

Bryan stepped back and looked into Kendra's eyes. "You want a separation?"

Separation. Hearing the word was worse than she'd anticipated. "No. I don't want a separation. I thought you wanted one. You left me and went to live with your brother. And even before that, whenever we were together at the townhouse, it felt more like cohabitating than living together in marriage. And it seemed that you hated being with me."

He took her hand in both of his. "No. I had to move out. I was filled with anger. Not at you. I was infuriated at the financial predicament I caused us by taking off work and sticking you with the bills for two years. Every time I saw you settling the checkbook, I felt horrible. And, when I watched you writing lesson plans and grading papers, I was jealous. I missed being in class, teaching students rather than staring at books day and night. And mostly, I realized how stupid it was for me to throw myself into a degree I didn't really need. So, I lashed out at everybody. I never really wanted to sell the beach house in the first place, but those words popped out of my mouth without thinking."

"So now what?" Kendra asked.

"I don't want to live apart from you ever again. Starting now. This summer. Here at the beach. That was why Felicia Wilson was trying to reach you. I asked her to take the cottage off the market, but she needed your approval to cancel the contract." He dropped to a knee, as though proposing. "So, do you accept me as your penitent husband, to have and to hold, from this day forward?"

Kendra thought of her wish. *I want my life back.* Here it was, within her grasp like a gift from a fairy godmother. "But what about your dissertation?"

"Finished, thank God. I turned it in yesterday. Dr. Miller had me sit in his office as he paged through the sections, checking formatting and the first paragraph of each chapter. I was a nervous wreck, of course. But he gave his approval. The only thing left between me and my diploma is my dissertation presentation and defense." He remained on bended knee.

She reached out her hand to him. "I do."

"What?"

"I do accept you as my husband. No penitence necessary."

Bryan stood up and kissed her. "During the entire drive

from College Park, I was nervous about this conversation. I thought I might be too late to tell you how I feel. I was afraid you didn't want to be with me anymore. I've been such a jerk lately."

"Yeah, you have." She smiled to let him know that she appreciated his mea culpa. "But I never stopped loving you, even when I hated you at the same time. And I've been crazy moody lately, too. That whole fertility thing with all those hormones bouncing around and messing with my emotions. But I've finally come to accept that I'm not going to be a mommy."

"Don't ever give up, Kendra. We can try again. We have all summer to be together here. My dissertation defense isn't scheduled until September. I plan to sit and stare at the ocean and let my mind and body rest. That way, my little guys will be more energized and might do their job."

"How do you know that it's your swimmers at fault and not a problem with my body?" Her mind leapt from infertility, to cancer, to whether or not to tell Bryan about her trip to the GI doctor. If it were cancer, how would Bryan handle watching her go through all that his mother had battled until the very end. No, she'd wait until after the colonoscopy. "I'm glad that—"

Her phone rang. The caller ID flashed the doctor's office number. She hoped that he wasn't postponing her colonoscopy; she couldn't bear to wait even longer.

"Kendra, I have the results from your blood tests and there's something that—" He stopped in midsentence. "You're not driving, are you?"

Her hands were shaking. "No, I'm home with my husband. Let me put you on speaker." Kendra's nausea returned. She let go of the phone and darted outside to the cool air on the back deck, leaving Bryan to deal with the news alone. She let the sound of the ocean waves calm her. She knew she was being a coward, but she didn't think she could keep it together.

Moments later, Bryan joined her on the deck. He held the phone in one hand and wiped his eyes with the back of his other hand.

She blinked back tears. "It's cancer, isn't it?"

"What? No. What made you think it was cancer?"

"If it's not cancer, then what is it?"

He put his arm around her shoulder and kissed her cheek. "Kendra, you're pregnant."

"What? How in the world?"

A voice came from the phone in Bryan's hand. "One of your blood tests showed the presence of the hCG hormone. It's an unmistakable sign of pregnancy."

Bryan handed her the phone.

"It's really not cancer? Then why—"

"Pregnancy would explain all your symptoms. Congratulations."

She rushed into Bryan's arms so suddenly that the cell phone flew from her hand to the sand below the deck, yet neither Bryan nor Kendra cared.

"We're going to be parents. How scary is that?" she asked. During all those years of trying to get pregnant, parenthood had been an idea, like playing house, but now she saw the enormity of what lay ahead.

"You'll be a great mom. I'll be the one who needs help with this parenting thing," Bryan said.

"We'll get through it together. Everyone does."

She breathed in the salty air and felt the tension start to

leave her body. Then, a thought popped into her mind, "Bryan, we have to go to dinner at Dirty Harry's tonight, okay?"

"You know I love the food there," he said, "but why not go somewhere fancy, like a steak house, to celebrate?"

"Not tonight." Kendra couldn't wait to tell Jean, the waitress, that she was right.

She and her hubby were expecting.

Paddleboarding Wasn't on Her Bucket List

If asked, Dani would never name paddleboarding as a bucket list item. For one thing, she'd never seen a paddleboard; for another, she didn't believe in having a bucket list. So, how did a paddleboard change her life?

Every summer, *Weekend Warrior Ideas* magazine shut down the offices for two weeks for "off-site adventures." Staff members were encouraged to use that vacation time to sample locations and activities to pitch at the brainstorming sessions held in November.

Dani was on a team of four. Initially strangers, they had become close friends during the past five years and now found time each week to do something together like try a new fusion restaurant or see an edgy art film. But when it came time for the off-site adventures, Celia, Vince, and Jack wanted something more exotic and daring.

Despite Dani's pink pixie haircut and sapphire contact lenses, she was not what you could call *gutsy*. She would rather edit and catalog digital images from faraway lands than actually visit those lands. She wished she were braver. She'd have loved skiing the Alps with Vince and then sipping hot brandy and cuddling with him in front of a stone fireplace. A fantasy, of course, since he wasn't even aware that she thought of him as more than a friend. In the meantime, she had already prepared her fake reason for not going on the next adventure and was ready to decline their invitation.

But this year, there had been no mention of the plans, and although she felt left out, she didn't dare bring up the topic.

On the last day before the two-week break, Dani heard Celia's muffled giggle behind her. "Guess where you're going to be tomorrow?"

Dani's heart started to race. "At home finishing up the digital files for next month's issue."

She turned and saw that her teammates were standing with their hands behind their backs, an obvious sign that they were up to something.

"Too late. The trip is already set." Celia held out the list she'd been hiding: Bathing suit, shorts, tank tops, sundress, flip-flops, PJs, sunblock, toiletries. "And, no, you can't stay here on photo duty."

"But where?" she asked.

"Here's a hint," Vince said with a wink. "A beach town often referred to as 'The Nation's Summer Capitol.'"

"Rehoboth Beach?" Although she had never visited coastal Delaware, Dani had edited photographs of the polar bear plunges that took place along the coast of Delmarva to support Special Olympics.

"Should we consider that a *yes*?" Celia asked. "Finally?"

"Yes." What could possibly be dangerous or scary at a Delaware beach?

"Well, thank God you said yes, or this would have been a foolish purchase," Vince said, revealing a bottle of Dom Pérignon, as Zack distributed the four champagne glasses he had held behind his back.

The next morning marked the start of Dani's first vacation with her work friends. The comfort she felt about the destination made the drive to Rehoboth joyous despite the heavy traffic over the Bay Bridge that became slower and heavier as they got closer to Rehoboth.

After dropping their luggage into the hotel rooms Vince had arranged, the four friends munched pizza and sipped craft beers at the Grotto Beach Bar on the boardwalk while Zack led a planning meeting on what to do, what to see, and where to eat. The ideas for their ten days at the beach spilled out at the same enthusiastic speed as when the four of them brainstormed concepts at *Weekend Warrior Ideas*.

All the suggestions were tame enough for Dani, until Zack looked past her toward the ocean and said, "Paddleboarding. We've gotta try that."

Vince and Zack high-fived, but Dani froze.

"Dani, it looks easy enough," said Celia. She pointed to a slender, redheaded woman, standing on what looked like a surfboard, just past the breakers. "See? How hard can it be? She looks totally Zen."

"Zen? Just because she French-braids her hair?" Dani watched the woman, whose board seemed to float over the ocean.

Zack scribbled "paddleboarding" at the top of the things-to-do list, and Vince asked the bartender if he knew where they could rent boards and get a lesson.

The guy answered, "I get that question all the time." He reached under the bar and handed them a colorful postcard. The front of the card showed a line of five teens, standing on boards and paddling along the beach with an azure sky as the backdrop. Contact information for the instructor was printed at the bottom.

Zack made the phone call. "Loreen? I'm calling about private paddleboard lessons ... Actually, four of us ... Beginners." He mouthed, *she sounds hot*, and Celia jabbed him in his ribs. "Tomorrow morning, the state park beach by Gordons Pond. Where's that?" The bartender flipped the card over. There was map of downtown Rehoboth and a red line down the streets that led to the entrance to that part of Henlopen State Park. "Never mind. Got it. And you supply the boards? ... Great! See you then."

Dani shivered, and Vince put his arm around her. "You'll be fine. You'll have all of us to take care of you. Have we ever let you down?" Or at least that's what she thought she heard. She was too focused on his closeness to notice his words.

At dinner that night, her friends avoided any mention of the paddleboarding lesson scheduled for the next day, but Dani couldn't forget. She continued to refill her wine glass, hoping to wake up sick and stay in the hotel room. "Worshipping the porcelain god" (as they called it in college) seemed preferable to drowning.

Her effort was futile. The next morning, Dani awoke to the sun streaming through the sheer curtains of the hotel room and a stomach that refused to play a part in her scheme.

Celia, already in a bikini top and surf shorts, jumped on Dani's bed. "Wake up, sleepyhead, and put on your swimsuit. Vince and Zack are getting pastries and coffee for the four of us and will meet us at the car. We have a date with paddleboarding, remember?"

"How could I forget?" She groaned, already imagining embarrassing herself in front of her work friends, but especially Vince.

At the Gordons Pond parking area, Dani leaned against the car while her friends lined up to be assigned paddles and boards that the instructor, Loreen, distributed after sizing up each of her students. Then Loreen called over to Dani, "You're next."

Dani responded, "I think I'll just hang out on the beach."

"Why? Are you afraid to try it?"

"I'm not much of a swimmer. And I have crappy balance."

"All my beginning students wear flotation vests, so the ability to swim is not an issue. And as for balance? I brought the wide boards that are designed for paddleboard yoga and, therefore, are more forgiving. Besides, saltwater provides buoyancy, so you'll do okay."

Celia, Vince, and Zack had already suited up in their flotation vests. Vince carried one over to her. "Come on, Dani, try it. None of us knows what we're doing. Besides, safety in numbers. Each of us has a whole team of rescuers if we fall off." He handed her the vest. "Like the Nike slogan says, 'Just do it.' And if you fall or freak out, I volunteer to come back to the beach with you. Okay?" His smile was reassuring.

Zack—being smart-ass rather than helpful—said, "Hey, paddleboarding on the ocean is definitely easier than a zip line in Peru or the double-diamond trails in the Alps," referring to adventures that her three friends had shared on past vacations without her.

Dani was relieved to hear they would start by learning the basics on the sand. Loreen covered terminology and demonstrated getting up on the board, three basic paddle moves, and how to safely fall from the board. "Tether the board leash to your ankle. It'll keep the board within easy reach if you do fall into the water." She handed out lanyards, each holding a bright orange whistle. "This is in case you have a problem. Blow the whistle to alert us so we can come to your aid."

It all seemed easy enough—and safe enough—for Dani to consider taking the full paddleboarding lesson. She followed Loreen and the others into waist-deep water just beyond the breakers, where they climbed onto their boards and into the starting position, kneeling in the center near the board's handle. A little scarier, but still manageable.

When they tried to go from kneeling to standing, everyone was wobbly, yet no one fell. Dani took a deep breath and exhaled. In her mind, the first real hurdle had passed, and she had been successful.

Loreen smiled. "Excellent! Shall we paddle? Imitate my strokes and stay in a straight line, leaving space in between so there's room just in case one of you does wipe out. No need to have a domino effect, right?"

Dani felt the blood drain from her face. She had assumed they'd just be trying out the moves here in the state park. "We're going somewhere?"

"Of course. We'll paddle to downtown Rehoboth. That's enough for most beginners. When we can see the bandstand part of the boardwalk, we'll sit on our boards for a tiny rest, and then we'll paddle back here." She focused on Dani. "If you get tired sooner than that, blow your whistle, and I can get you to shore, where your friends can pick you up after the lesson."

Zack followed Loreen, and Celia followed him.

Vince suggested that Dani go behind Celia so he could stay in the back, in case she needed help, but she was afraid that her slowness would frustrate the group. "I'll be fine. I'd rather not stress about my speed of paddling. As Loreen said, if I need help, I'll just ..." She held up the orange whistle. Truthfully, she didn't want Vince to see how unathletic she was.

Vince smiled and gave a thumbs-up, but Dani thought he seemed disappointed as he paddled into place behind Celia. She hoped she hadn't hurt his feelings, though she'd given a perfectly acceptable reason for wanting to be at the end of the line.

The group paddled parallel to the shoreline. Though it was obvious that Loreen's students were all first-time paddleboarders, they stayed afloat, and the line continued to move forward.

Dani saw that the distance between her and Vince was lengthening, but she refused to blow the whistle. She was determined not to wreck anyone's fun today, nor would she allow herself to quit so easily. When she was almost at the northern end of the boardwalk, the others were at least three blocks farther along. Fortunately, everyone was concentrating on paddling so intently that they didn't notice this. Dani, on the other hand, needed a distraction to keep her from thinking about her balance. She glanced at the families on the beach and at a group of youngsters splashing in the water.

A woman, who was a bit too large for a bikini, stood up and called out toward the water, "Mikey, get back here," with the stern voice of a frustrated mother.

A young boy about ten years old, wearing a surfer-dude T-shirt, was holding tightly to a boogie board and kicking his feet to catch a swell of water that was building into a tall breaker. Dani wondered, *Is this Mikey?*

She stopped paddling and kept her eyes on the boy, who was between her and the swimmers closer to shore. He and his board were lifted high into the air. Then, the wave broke and sent him headfirst into the water. His boogie board flew up into the air, and he disappeared.

The bikinied mother screamed, "Mikey! Oh my God! Somebody! Help!"

Lifeguard whistles filled the air, and the lifeguards rushed into action, two of them sprinting to the water and another one keeping the other beachgoers out of the way.

The boy reappeared, popping up and down in the water, not showing any evidence of knowing how to swim. Instinctively, Dani knelt on her board and paddled frantically toward him. She tried to pull the boy onto her board, but she didn't have the arm strength, so she jumped off her board and held the boy tightly, letting her flotation vest hold them both up.

The two lifeguards arrived.

One lifeguard immediately took charge of the boy and started taking him toward the beach while Mikey screeched, "My boogie board! Where's my boogie board?"

The other lifeguard, who had a dragon tattoo that wrapped over his left shoulder, called out, "I'll get it." But he stayed for a moment with Dani. "Great save."

That was the moment Dani realized that she had jumped into the water without hesitation. When her brain comprehended what she had done, her body began shivering.

"Are you going to be okay?" the lifeguard asked.

She nodded.

"I guess I'd better retrieve the kid's board before he escapes his mom and runs into the surf to find it. Maybe next time he won't be lucky enough to have a paddleboarder ready to save his butt."

As the lifeguard swam for the wayward boogie board, Dani tried to get back onto her paddleboard. It had been easy in the waist-high water where they'd practiced. But here, in the deeper water, it was tougher than she'd expected. She tried throwing her leg over the board, but that didn't work. She tried to fling her arms over the board, but it was too wide for her grasp. She blew the orange whistle.

It caught the attention of the tattooed lifeguard. He rushed toward her with the boogie board in tow. "Need help?"

Vince arrived seconds later, his eyes filled with worry. "Dani. Are you okay?"

She looked from the sexy lifeguard to her secret crush. "I just can't seem to get back up. I understand how to do it—in theory—but I've never actually climbed back onboard in water deeper than my waist."

"Beginner? No way. You saved that kid's life." the lifeguard said.

Before the lifeguard could assist Dani, Vince left his

own board. "I've got you, Dani." He swam behind her and placed his hands on her waist. "When I lift you, grab the handle in the center of the board with your dominant hand and pull yourself up."

She succeeded and settled into a seated position. "Thanks, Vince." She wanted to call him her hero, but that would be too silly.

The lifeguard pointed to the other three paddleboarders heading toward them, Loreen in front and at full speed, while her two remaining students struggled with balance versus speed. "Looks like the cavalry is on its way."

Not much of a cavalry, considering that both Celia and Zack fell off their boards.

Loreen continued without them. "Hi, Keith," she said to the lifeguard. "Is she okay?"

But it was Vince who answered, "She's more than okay. She saved a kid's life."

"Seriously? That's pretty brave for someone who didn't want to paddleboard today."

The lifeguard nodded toward Loreen's other students. "Do you need my help getting them back on their boards?"

"Nah," she said. "Haven't you heard the expression *learn by doing*?"

As the lifeguard swam toward shore with the kid's boogie board, Loreen, Vince, and Dani watched Celia get back on her board and try to pull Zack out of the water.

"Grab the handle in the center!" Dani yelled out.

Loreen clapped her hands. "Fast learner."

The compliment was appreciated, but Dani was more rewarded by Vince's dimpled smile.

After their first adventure as a team, something changed. There was an altered energy among them. Not a bad feeling, but something intense. She noticed that Zack and Celia often stood together in private talk. About what? And Dani was uber-aware of Vince. Was she being overly excited by his frequent smiles in her direction? She questioned her interpretation of all of this but didn't have long to wait for the answer.

At dinner, Zack and Celia accidentally revealed that they'd been dating. When Celia expressed concern that her relationship with Zack might impact future vacations, or at least the rooming aspect, Vince touched Dani's hand and said, "We're all adults here. I'm sure we can work things out."

Dani felt her cheeks warm. Vince was holding her hand. She replayed those few minutes on the paddleboards when Vince came to rescue her. She thought of all the things he'd said and the ways he'd acted since they arrived in Rehoboth. Everything seemed to point to a connection between them that went beyond being work buddies. She hoped her gut feeling was right. "So where are we going next year?"

"That depends on you," Vince said. "The time we've spent here at the beach has been great, and now I can't imagine a trip without you along. So, where would you be willing to travel next year?"

She thought for a moment. She wanted to say, "anywhere, as long as you're with me," but she thought it best to keep the conversation light and save more intimate discussions for later, when she and Vince could be alone.

During the wait, Zack said, "It doesn't need to be an *Amazing Race* type of vacation. This trip to Rehoboth was better than spelunking in the caves of Mexico or rock climbing in France." His face, however, displayed hope that she would show interest in one of those adventures.

But romance was on her mind. *Paris? No. Too busy. Italy?* She lifted her wine glass into the air. "There's always a sipping tour of the Tuscany vineyards."

Vince caught Dani's subtext. "I'll drink to that!"

"And stay at a bed and breakfast in the countryside," Dani added, glancing at Vince.

A smile broke across his face.

Zack busily googled B&Bs in Tuscany, while Celia leaned in to see the screen on his phone.

Vince whispered to Dani, "I hope you aren't going to make me wait a year."

Without hesitation, Dani said, "How about a walk on the beach?"

Zack looked up from his phone. "What a great idea!"

But Celia nudged him and said, "She wasn't talking to us, dummy."

Dani stood and held out her hand to Vince.

He tossed his credit card to Zack, "This meal is on me."

Together, Dani and Vince headed toward the beach and horizons well beyond it.

The Healing Power of Feeding Seagirls

Kara woke to a growling stomach. She wished she'd done some grocery shopping before coming to this beach condo, but she had been exhausted after the long drive yesterday from Wheaton, Maryland, to Bethany Beach, Delaware. She hadn't even unpacked yet. Instead, she had fallen across the bed and into a deep sleep.

Barb, a dear friend who owned the dental practice where Kara was a hygienist, had sent her here. "Bethany Beach. It will be a healing retreat."

I doubt it, Kara had thought. She questioned whether time at a beach could repair the gaping hole she felt inside.

The events of last week sprang to life yet again.

When her doorbell had rung early in the morning and she opened the door, the sight of two uniformed members of the armed services, both with their hats held to their chests, had brought her life to a screeching halt. She couldn't talk. She couldn't even cry. She could only feel her heart break. She nodded and indicated that they could come into the house. She led them to the living room, where she slowly lowered herself onto her husband Mark's favorite chair—probably the worst choice she could have made. As she sank into the soft brown corduroy, she sobbed uncontrollably and unabashedly to the point of hyperventilation. One of the soldiers brought her a glass of water while the other (an army chaplain) knelt beside her and handed her his handkerchief.

The next morning, after the news channels released the names of the four soldiers who had died, her phone rang and rang and rang until she finally shut it off.

Not able to reach her, Barb left the office and drove to Kara's house. Barb assured her that her patients would be covered, then offered Kara her condo in Bethany Beach. A quiet haven for the entire month of June. "It's just a tiny efficiency on the second floor of an old beach house, but it's only two blocks from the boardwalk and beach."

Kara saw a half-drunk bottle of ginger ale she'd left out on the counter last night. It should have been put into the fridge, but at room temperature, it tasted okay and would hopefully be enough until she reached a café where she could order breakfast and a strong coffee.

She sipped the flat soda as she sat by the window that overlooked the yard of the house that backed up to the property. On the porch of that house, an elderly woman in a summer housedress sat at a wicker table across from a small, red-haired child wearing a blue denim romper. Between them, a silver tray held a floral china tea set.

The woman's tea ritual mesmerized Kara. The delicate tongs that lifted cubed sugar to the teacup, the tilt of the cream pitcher, the swirl of the spoon. She envied the child for having this time with a grandparent. Kara wished her "Grams" were alive. Grams could heal her with the strength of a kiss on top of a Band-Aid.

The memory was too much for Kara. She slipped into her sandals and set out in search of food and a freshly brewed cup of coffee.

At the corner of Pennsylvania Avenue and Garfield Parkway, she found Beach Break Bakrie and Café. With a large coffee in one hand and a sticky bun in the other, she wandered down the main street toward the boardwalk and beach, glancing at the shop windows on her way. She stopped at the four-window corner of Bethany Beach Books and looked inside at the book displays. She scanned the groupings of books and wondered what she'd want to read. At any other time in her life, she would have chosen a romance, but not today. Maybe a book of comic essays. Something to make her laugh and escape this summer of sadness. With her right hand messy from the sticky bun, she couldn't go inside. Maybe later, after she washed her hands.

After cleaning up in the public restrooms on the boardwalk at the end of Garfield, she found an empty bench and sat facing the ocean with her feet propped up against the wooden railing that separated the boardwalk from the sand dune engineered to keep the ocean from flooding the stores during nor'easters.

A seagull positioned itself at her feet. *Dumb bird,* she almost said aloud. *I don't have anything to eat. You're wasting your time.* "Shoo!"

She hated seagulls. When she was twelve, a seagull had deposited a messy dropping on her favorite beach towel; she had never used that towel again, even though her mom insisted that the washing machine had "made it all new again." *Oh, for a washing machine that could make* me *new again.*

The white-blue sky was almost cloudless, and the sun was already warming the sand. She watched a young family with two little boys head toward the steps that led down to the beach. One was pulling at his mom's arm, straining to get to the beach sooner, while the other was riding piggyback on his dad, who had his arms filled with beach chairs and an umbrella. It made Kara think of Mark's arms. How he worked out. How he could bench press her. How safe she used to feel in his embrace. How he would have been a great daddy for their kids. *If only we hadn't waited to get pregnant.*

Her eyes burned, not from the sun, but because she refused to cry again. To give in to grief would be to accept that Mark was gone. She wasn't ready to concede that unavoidable truth.

A high-pitched voice called out, "Granny, here, here!" The child plopped on the bench beside her. Kara recognized the denim romper and bright hair, now neatly braided. This was the little girl she'd seen from the window of the condo.

The grandmother approached the bench and said to the little girl, "Elise, did you ask the nice lady if she would mind sharing the bench?"

Elise looked into Kara's face, then back to her grandmother. "Why?"

The woman leaned over and in a soft voice explained, "Because it's the polite thing to do."

"Oh." Then, "Miss, can me and Granny sit here?"

Kara wanted to be alone, but she knew that someone

would eventually sit on the empty half of the bench. These two were as good a choice as any. Besides, the woman reminded her of a happy time in her life—a time spent with her Grams. "Of course, you can sit here." She almost said, "can sit here with me," but that would invite conversation, something that she didn't intend to suggest.

The woman opened a bag of bread crumbs and the purpose of their visit became clear. They were there to feed the seagulls, an idea that made Kara regret her consent. At the first toss of food over the railing, gulls gathered on the top of the dune as though they were extras in a remake of Hitchcock's *The Birds*. She weighed how soon she could leave the bench without being rude.

"They're always so happy to see us," the elderly woman said.

Elise offered Kara a handful of crumbs. "Would you like to feed the sea girls, too?"

Sea girls? It was cute. As was Elise. Cute.

Kara had always imagined that she and Mark would have boys, but the bright green eyes of this little girl presented a new image—her husband lifting Elise on his shoulders so she could toss the bread higher into the air. *Daddy's Little Girl.*

She shouldn't have let her mind go there. She stared out at the ocean, refusing to let her eyelids move. She didn't need to look down to know that the little girl had moved closer.

"This is for you," Elise said.

Kara could see the little hand reaching up and holding out a piece of bread.

The first tears escaped and, once released, the rest poured in a torrent. She could no longer contain her emotions. "I'm sorry," she managed to say, aware that the little girl was staring at her.

"Why is she crying?" the child asked.

The grandmother handed the bag of bread crumbs to her. "Elise. Go down on the beach and spread these a little farther so more of your sea girls can eat."

Elise obeyed and skipped down the walkway and the stairs to the open sand.

Then the woman turned to Kara. "Is there anything I can do for you?"

She wasn't Grams, but that didn't matter. The words rushed out. About Mark. About how he and three other soldiers died in an airplane crash—not shot down over a battlefield but crashed over a military airfield as a result of mechanical failure. Not that the reason mattered. He was gone. When Kara had exhausted the details of last week, she spoke about her marriage to the "most wonderful man in the world." She opened her cell phone and located a photo of LTC Mark Anderson. "He was smart. And brave. And funny. And kind." She smiled, but only for a moment. "And now I'm all alone." She looked up at the sky and asked, "What do I do now?" She took a deep breath, then exhaled slowly, ending in small burst of *ahhh*.

The woman, who had listened in silence until Kara's words stumbled into that sigh, answered, "You know in your heart what needs to be done. Surely, as your husband was a smart, brave, funny, and kind man, he wouldn't want you to live in the Land of Regrets. I know it's easy for me to say this, but you must be brave, too. You must go forward."

Kara wiped her eyes with her T-shirt sleeves. "But how?"

The woman gazed at the beach where her grandchild

was dancing in the sand under a shower of bread crumbs. "So many people hate the seagulls. My husband, Henry, insisted we feed them; he reminded me, and anyone else who would listen, that the gulls are God's creatures, too. When my Henry died, I stopped saving bread for the gulls. I avoided the beach and stayed home with my grief. Then, one morning when I walked to the mailbox, I saw a sparrow tugging at a worm to feed its young. That's when I finally cried. And my tears brought a clarity I'd been missing for months. I realized how, in trying to bury my pain, I'd buried everything that had ever made me happy. I'd buried everything that was good about my Henry. So, I feed the gulls again, and I teach Elise what Henry taught me."

Kara appreciated the story shared by this stranger, this substitute for her own wise grandmother. It reminded her of the importance of family, including extended family like her friend Barb. "Is your granddaughter visiting for the summer?"

The woman shook her head. "No. Elise lives here year-round. Her parents are gone. She was a baby, too young to remember them or the accident. Miraculously, she was unharmed when the drunk driver hit their car head-on. I do my best to protect her innocent joy. I hope I'm blessed with enough years to see her off to college. In the meantime, I live in the present, trying to make each day special."

Elise rushed up to her grandmother. "All done."

"All done," her grandmother repeated. Then, to Kara, "It's never easy. But after the tears, and acceptance of the truth, the hill isn't so hard to climb anymore." The woman stood, brushed a few stray crumbs from her skirt, and took her grandchild's hand.

Kara watched the elderly lady as she ambled down the boardwalk with the little girl. She imagined a Henry walking next to them and almost believed that she saw the outline of just such a man in the air beside the old woman. A daydream, of course, but comforting.

She felt a flutter near her feet. A sparrow landed and grabbed one of the crumbs that had fallen on the boardwalk. It looked up at her before it flew away, tilting its head from side to side as though trying to figure her out. "Are you Henry's sparrow?" she asked the bird.

Kara felt a warm breeze flow over her body from head to toe, though there was very little movement in the sea grass that separated the boardwalk from the beach. For a second, she wondered how that was possible—feeling what didn't exist—but something from deep inside implored her to just gratefully accept any gentle reminder of the love she'd shared with Mark.

Standing Up in the Limo

A beach wedding. A first wedding for the bride-to-be. The excitement of buying the dream gown and planning the big event. The happiest time of her life, right? Should have been. Would have been. If. If she were in her twenties. If she were a size eight.

But Alice was neither.

She had just turned fifty. Her clothing size wavered between twelve and fourteen, although her five-foot-eight height made her look thinner than either of those sizes. She accepted the gray strands that were creeping into her brunette hair, but she kept her hair long rather than cut it short like so many women do when they reach "a certain age."

So, how did she arrive at this moment, standing in the opened moonroof of a limo, wearing a plastic tiara with the word "Bride" in large flashing letters, and waving like the Queen of England?

She had never expected to get engaged, especially once she had fully accepted that her life would be lived out as a single woman. Her career as a Wall Street analyst, working with the powerful Walter Joseph Illian, validated her as someone to be respected and not felt sorry for. Sure, she had been in love before, but only in that secret place of one's heart, where things are stored but never shared. The crush on a dentist. The fascination with a cute guy who sat nearby in the college lecture hall. The obsession with a street musician who played in the subway station she used. And Mr. Illian. Not really a crush, but more a deep platonic friendship. After all, he was in his early nineties. *Was.*

An unexpected inheritance from her nonagenarian client made her see the world of Wall Street through different eyes. No other client inspired her to remain in such a high-pressured job. She chose early retirement and bought a summer place in Dewey, Delaware, in an ocean-side development in which Mr. Illian had invested money. It became her full-time residence five years ago when she decided to spend more time with the friends she'd made during her summer vacations there.

Since her move to coastal Delaware, Alice's social life had expanded. She enjoyed a great circle of friends who did everything together—walking, bowling, golfing, crafting, and just sitting on the beach under a cluster of umbrellas. They called themselves the Dewey Dames. She was the youngest by twelve years and was the only one not on Medicare. Age didn't matter; the fun they had together did.

But still, she was lonely sometimes. So, when she saw a news story on TV about the Delaware Humane Association's new adoption site in Midway Plaza, Alice realized what was missing in her life. Ginger. Not ginger spice or ginger ale. Ginger, a domestic shorthair cat with whom she had shared her condo in New York. Every afternoon when Alice came home from her job, she'd find Ginger lying on the table by the front window, watching the activities on East 83rd. The cat would look up at her, wait for a gentle rub, and then go back to observing the outdoor world. Ginger was as self-sufficient as Alice, and that made her an excellent pet. Sadly, Ginger had passed away. The loneliness that followed was like the loneliness she'd been experiencing lately. She needed a feline roommate again.

The next day, she visited the adoption center and fell in love with a tiny orange-and-white kitten that looked a lot like her former pet. "Maybe it's a sign that I should adopt her," she told the volunteer.

"Of course, you're free to adopt," the volunteer replied, "but give it a day or two before committing. A new kitten can't replace the bond you had with Ginger, and she probably won't have the same personality. Be sure that you're taking home a kitten for the right reason and this isn't an impulsive decision."

That afternoon, a.k.a. Tee-Time Tuesday, Alice joined her friends for a few rounds of miniature golf. The Dewey Dames usually played three rounds at Shell We Golf and then enjoyed coffee and sweets at Starbucks, but Alice couldn't stop talking about the kitten—and cats in general—and the others, who were not cat fans, putted with such rapid, fierce strokes that their first round went quicker than usual.

"Wow, that went fast," Margo said.

Elaine tapped her golf club against the ground as they returned to the first hole for their second round of golf. "Because someone in our little group couldn't shut up about cats."

Alice was embarrassed by the realization that she had indeed been talking nonstop. "Okay. I'm sorry. I'm just so excited at the prospect of sharing my condo with a companion again."

"Companion?" Elaine snorted. "It's a cat, for crap's sake."

Sharon jumped in. "Can we just play golf?" She smacked the yellow ball so hard it bounced off the green and onto the walkway.

"Okay. That's it," Elaine said. "Time for an intervention, before we have a cat lady on our hands."

The other ladies watched Elaine carry her golf club to the return counter and then touch a speed-dial number on her cell phone. "Good morning to you, too. I know this is last minute, but it is middle of the week and the middle of a sunny day when everybody will be on the beach, so I think you can make this work. My friends and I need emergency mani-pedis … Five of us … I know, I know, but the tip will be worthy of working your magic … Of course, we'll take anyone who's available. Everyone on staff is highly qualified … In an hour? How about if we arrive a bit earlier and sit outside on the second-floor deck? … Excellent. See you soon."

Elaine returned to the group with a bright smile on her face. "Bad Hair Day. Told them we have an emergency. Margo, we should all pile into your SUV. You know how difficult it is to find a parking spot during the summer season."

"Of course," Margo said.

As they piled into the vehicle, Elaine said, "But first, we stop at Outlet Liquors."

Sharon raised her eyebrows. "Aren't you forgetting that the salon offers free wine?"

"Duh. Of course I haven't forgotten. I just know that I want more than one glass of wine, and apparently, so do you, Sharon, based on how hard you smacked that golf ball. I don't want the salon to run out of everything they have. We certainly don't want to become unwelcome at our favorite place to unwind."

During the drive, Margo laid down some rules. "A reminder of the rules of intervention: One—This is not an attack on you, Alice; it is our effort as your friends to express our concerns for your well-being, and you must simply listen and not say anything until we are done. Two—Everyone can say one thing, and only one thing, to let Alice know we care about her and why we felt the need for an intervention. Three—If someone has nothing extra to add, she will simply say, 'Ditto.' Four—After we've all had the opportunity to express our words of concern, then we may each suggest a solution to the problem. And finally—We will not step foot into Bad Hair Day until the intervention is complete. Our mani-pedis are a time of relaxation and joy. Got it?"

Alice looked around as her friends nodded in assent, and the intervention began.

The Dewey Dames felt that Alice needed a guy in her life, not a cat. They told horror stories about people they'd known who started with one cat, then another, and another, while becoming more and more isolated. They claimed that having a pet would affect her marriage prospects—What if she met the man of her dreams and he was allergic to cats or hated pets in general? Was she willing to rehome the cat, and could she forgive herself if she did that? Then came the solutions. Suggestions that Alice volunteer at the DHA so she could have time with cats without owning one. That she add some evening activities to get her out of the house during the time most associated with elder loneliness. And that they try out new venues on their Thursday Thirst-Quenching (a.k.a. enjoying adult beverages while chatting the day away) to expand the possibilities for her finding an available guy to date.

"But I don't want to date," she insisted.

"Of course, you do," Elaine said.

Connie added, "My late husband was barely in the grave when Elaine tried to fix me up."

Elaine defended her actions. "It was for your own good, Connie. Your Justin would have wanted you to be happy." She turned the focus back onto Alice. "We cannot stand by and watch you throw all your love into a cat. You deserve a good man."

By the time the intervention was done, and Operation Halt Cat-Lady Syndrome began, Alice needed wine and the mani-pedi more than her friends.

The next day, Alice bowed out of their Wednesday Walking. She told them she had some errands to run, promised she would get enough exercise, and told them that one of her errands was to inquire about volunteering at the DHA.

She waited impatiently in the northbound traffic from Dewey but managed to arrive at the center by eleven, only to discover it was closed on Wednesdays. Like a parent looking into a hospital nursery, she glanced through the large window and watched the cats resting on furniture or playing. In the far corner, she saw that the kitten she had wanted to adopt was still there. Her heart melted. How could she not adopt that orange-and-white fluff of fur?

Her decision was made. Ginger 2.0 was officially going to be hers. *Look at the positive,* she said to herself. *I can use this time to shop for cat essentials and make my condo kitten-friendly before I bring home the baby.* Baby? *Maybe my friends are right. Is this the dangerous edge of the cliff, where I might indeed become a crazy cat lady?* She shrugged it off. *That's ridiculous. I wasn't a cat lady in New York. Or was I? After all, I'm the only one in the group who has remained single. When was the last time I went on a date?*

The kitten left its place in the corner of the room and approached the window. It looked up at her with big blue eyes and opened its mouth in a soft meow. Alice melted. "You're coming home with me tomorrow—Ginny." The name was set. And so was Alice's plan: Tell no one about the adoption. Never speak about the cat when the Dewey Dames were around. Go along with her friends and be open to meeting new people. Accept date offers.

With time on her hands and the need to plan for the kitten, she did a stop-and-shop at several local pet supply stores in Rehoboth and Lewes. She filled her VW Beetle convertible with the necessities (bowls, food, sturdy travel carrier, scratching post, kitty sack bed, and a litter box from Concord Pet), accessories and fun items (collar with matching leash, treats, and toys from Pups of Lewes), and a soft cat carrier that looked more like a Louis Vuitton designer handbag from Critter Beach. She used to laugh at people who carried their tiny, pure-breed dogs in such handbags, but now she appreciated their desire for taking their pets along rather than leaving them home alone.

As she was leaving Critter Beach, Alice saw the other

four members of the Dewey Dames, heading up Rehoboth Avenue. She wasn't sure if they'd seen her, but she had to act quickly. She threw beach towels over the items on the back seat of her VW. Fortunately, she was parked in front of the TCBY and not directly in front of the pet store. She quickly ran into the frozen yogurt store and bought a Mrs. Field's chocolate chip cookie. Upon exiting the shop, she made a theatrical wave at the girls and crossed the street to meet up with them. "How was your walk? I was hoping I might catch up with you for some coffee, but first I needed a cookie fix."

They didn't have a clue that she was covering up her visit to the pet store and that she would be a kitten's human momma the next day.

While she was enjoying coffee and concealing her excitement about adopting Ginny, the unofficial leader of the Dewey Dames, Elaine, innocently added another obstacle to Alice's plans. "As tomorrow is Thursday Thirst-Quenching, I think we should act on our decision to try new places. Instead of hitting our favorite bar in Dewey, we should sample some bars in Rehoboth and Lewes. Let's meet at On the Rocks, outside the Lewes ferry terminal, for their happy hour. I hear it's lively."

Alice pretended to be thrilled at the suggestion, but inside she was worried about leaving the kitten home alone on its first day as her feline companion. "Darn," she said, as though just having realized something. "I can't make it. Not tomorrow. Maybe next week?"

"If your plans were that important, you wouldn't have so easily forgotten about them, so just cancel whatever," Elaine insisted. "I can pick you up at your house."

Alice wasn't going to get past this lioness of the Dewey Dames. "That won't be necessary. I'll meet you there."

"Tomorrow at four." Elaine smiled. "Maybe you'll meet the man of your dreams there. Who knows?"

The next morning, Alice couldn't wait to get to the DHA adoption center. Her condo was ready, and the sturdy cat carrier was on the passenger seat of her car. She waited at the door of the center, carrier in hand, until noon when the center was scheduled to open. While waiting, she made eye contact with the kitten. "Hi, sweetie," she said, tapping on the window.

When a volunteer at the center opened the door, Alice was bubbling over with enthusiasm. She was relieved that the kitten she'd fallen in love with had not been claimed and was immediately adoptable.

While she filled out the paperwork, her hand shook with excitement, and she told the volunteer about her life with Ginger in New York and how much she missed that wonderful companion.

The woman smiled, nodded, and said to her, "So, I'm guessing you know the ups and downs of being a pet parent. Is your home ready for …?"

"Ginny. I'm naming her Ginny. And, yes, my condo is kitten-ready safe and welcoming. I promise she will have the best life possible."

Ginny wasn't thrilled with being in a plastic carrier, but Alice had anticipated that and had placed a soft cushion and a cat treat inside. As she drove, Alice periodically wiggled her index finger through the wire door of the carrier and let the kitten bat at it as though it were a toy. This kept the kitten distracted while on the way to its new home in Dewey.

The afternoon happy hour came too fast for Alice. She had been enjoying every second with Ginny, playing with her and taking photographs and videos of her kitten's first day in its forever home. She held back a tear as she closed her pet inside the room with her litter box, where she would be safe while unchaperoned. It broke her heart to leave Ginny, but she had the Dewey Dames expecting her at On the Rocks, and she certainly didn't want them to suspect that she had become a one-cat lady.

In her desire to appear enthusiastic about joining her friends at this location, which they had chosen in hopes of finding available men for Alice, she arrived too early. She wasn't sure whether they intended to sit at a table or at the bar, so she waited, hoping one of the other ladies would be early, too.

As she stood by the entrance, she heard a voice from the bar call out, "Alice? Alice Dalton? Is that you?"

When she turned, she saw a man approaching her. His hair was black with silver running through it, but his green eyes gave away his identity. "Paul Evans?" He had been her ninth-grade boyfriend. They had been madly in love—the kind of love that freshmen in high school have. Unfortunately, his father was transferred, and the family moved to Missouri. Alice and Paul had written to each other for a while and had spoken on the phone the few times their parents allowed them a long-distance call, but eventually, their lives got busy with other friends and they lost touch.

"What are you doing here?" she asked.

"I bought a condo in Port Lewes." He gestured toward the line of townhouses that bordered the ferry terminal grounds. "Sometimes I walk over here for lunch or dinner. I can't get enough of their crab dip and the Ferry Dogs with all the trimmings." His face showed the same dimpled smile she remembered. "What are the chances we'd meet again, and in Delaware, where neither of us had grown up?" He gave her a big hug, during which time, he whispered to her, "There are some women behind you staring at us. Is it okay if I give you a big kiss so they really have something to talk about?"

She didn't want to turn around, but she suspected they were the rest of the Dewey Dames. "Sure. A big dramatic one like you gave me when we played Maria and Tony in our high school musical."

Despite the theatricality, his kiss sent goosebumps down her body. She reminded herself they were just playing a trick on her friends and that Paul was surely married by now.

"How about we sit together and catch up?" he asked.

She wished she could, but there was the matter of the Dewey Dames. "Those women behind me? They're probably the friends I'm meeting."

"I understand." Dimpled smile. "How about if you and I meet up this evening at Gilligan's for dinner at six?"

She agreed, of course.

As soon as Paul returned to his seat in the bar, her friends surrounded her. "Who's that?" and "Where'd he come from?" were the hushed questions as they were seated at an outdoor table.

But Connie's comment was Alice's favorite. "So, Elaine, does this mean we don't have to set up an online dating profile for her after all?"

"That depends on whether that gorgeous hunk is single, available, and ready to shower our friend with the affection and love that will protect her from becoming a cat-owning hermit," she answered.

Alice felt her face warm, not from the sunny day, but from a mixture of emotions. She explained that she and Paul had gone to school together in Baltimore and their reunion today was a total surprise to both of them. And, no, she didn't know his marital status or much of anything about his current life. She left out the part about meeting him later tonight.

"Well, why aren't you over there sitting with him? If he's married, he'll tell you, and if he's not married, he'll most likely tell you that, too," Elaine said.

"No. I'm here as a Dewey Dame."

Elaine tilted her head to the side, glancing over at Paul. "You know, Alice, the only reason we chose to switch drinking establishments was to open up the opportunity for you, and for Connie when she's ready, to find a life partner. We at this table totally understand and encourage you to walk right over there. If he's married, maybe he'll have a single friend and play matchmaker. That's better than having us girls send you on dates with strangers."

Alice wondered if she should just tell them that she and Paul had already set a dinner date, but she figured that she'd let Elaine feel victorious. "Okay. I'll go over there with Paul, but the Dewey Dames must agree to stop staring at us."

The deal was made, but when Alice stood, she noticed Paul was no longer sitting at the bar. She was disappointed and relieved at the same time—disappointed for obvious reasons, yet relieved that she and Paul would have the privacy of dinner together and, if a woman came to Gilligan's with him, she'd know what she needed to know without the embarrassment of asking.

She hated to leave Ginny alone again. She remembered the volunteer's words: *Be sure you're ready to care for this cat for the rest of its life.* So, she made sure she cuddled and played with Ginny before taking a shower and dressing for dinner. "I promise lots of love when I get back from dinner."

All the way to Gilligan's, her stomach was filled with butterflies. Would she be able to hide her disappointment if he had a wife with him? What would she say? And, if he came alone, how could she bring up the topic of availability without seeming ridiculously needy?

When she arrived at the restaurant, Paul was waiting for her. Alone. He led her to a waterfront table that he had arranged for them. Throughout dinner, dessert, and way too much wine, they chatted about their careers, their families, and what they enjoyed most in life. Paul talked about his recent move from the Midwest to Lewes after retiring early from the police department to follow his dream of running a recreational fishing boat; Alice talked about her life in New York working on Wall Street. She stifled a sigh of relief when Paul mentioned that his ex-wife, from whom he was divorced eleven years ago, lived in Missouri with his two grown sons. He looked likewise relieved when Alice talked about living the single life in Manhattan, dating often, yet never finding the right person.

"Maybe we were both looking for what we had found much earlier in life," he said.

She smiled and blushed, as she suddenly felt like a four-teen-year-old again. By the end of dinner, it was as though they'd never been apart.

Paul said, "Alice, I know this sounds like a pickup line, but you know me better than that, I think. I get the feeling that our being in the same place at the same time was not coincidental. It's as though we were meant to be reunited. Despite all the years apart, you and I still fit together, at least as friends. I'd like to spend more time with you. We can call it dating, though that sounds so juvenile. Would you be interested in spending time with me?" He looked for her reaction. "I feel like a teenaged boy asking a girl to the prom, something I always thought I'd be asking you if our paths hadn't pulled us apart at the start of sophomore year."

Alice grinned. "I'd love to finally be your prom date."

Her friends were thrilled that Alice was dating. And now that she could no longer be accused of becoming a cat lady, she shared that she had indeed adopted the kitten from DHA. Ginny. Surprisingly, the Dewey Dames accepted her cat ownership.

"So, we can assume that Paul isn't allergic?" Sharon asked.

She proudly responded, "He loads up on allergy meds rather than stay away."

The Dewey Dames were impressed that Alice's guy was willing to suffer allergy symptoms for her, surely a heroic act meant to show his strong commitment to their relationship. Whenever she joined them for weekday activities, they barraged her with questions about Paul. It was as though they were living vicariously through her rekindled romance.

At first, this was fun for both Alice and her friends, but as she spent more and more time with Paul, the Dewey Dames started to miss her. They missed her so much that they appeared at her doorstep one morning with bagels, cream cheese, and coffee from Surf Bagel.

Alice was holding the kitten when she opened the door.

"Surprise!" the ladies called out in unison.

"May we come in?" Elaine asked while scanning the room.

It was obvious to Alice that she was checking for any signs of an overnight guest. "Of course, you can."

They entered the condo, arranged the breakfast goodies on the kitchen counter and jumped into the animated conversations that had always been part of their weekday activities. They talked about anything and everything, but Alice noticed they avoided any mention of Paul; it seemed that they had agreed to keep the chat light and fun like it was before.

Three hours later, the ladies were talked out and, having moved from plain coffee to Kahlua-spiked coffee, were slightly tipsy. In the process, they had renewed their comradery and had reached a decision to be more flexible and less interfering with each other's lives outside the group.

Alice was happier than ever. She had great friends, her kitten roommate, Ginny, and a wonderful relationship with Paul. Life couldn't get any better than this, she thought. Yet, it could. After three months of dating, one starlit night in August, as she and Paul were sitting on the balcony of his townhouse, looking out at Delaware Bay and enjoying a bottle of pinot noir, he took her hand.

"Before I moved here, I had stopped believing in love. But the moment I saw you, I knew it was fate giving us another chance." He got down on one knee. "Alice Dalton, will you marry me?"

It was the question she never thought she would get. She had assumed the time for falling in love had passed her by. But it was the question she had secretly held in her heart since the day she and Paul were reunited. She took a deep breath and exhaled. "Yes. Yes, of course I'll marry you."

Paul brought out a robin-blue ring box and opened it, revealing a ring with a diamond solitaire. "Thank God," he said, as he placed it on her finger. "I was afraid to ask—terrified you'd say no, and my life would be over."

As she and the other Dewey Dames lined up for their Tuesday Tee-Time golf, Alice held up her left hand and let the sun's rays bounce off the diamond in her ring.

Connie was the first to notice. She squealed. "Is that what I think it is?"

Margo grabbed Alice's wrist. "Holy shit! An engagement ring!"

The rest of the girls dropped their putters and crowded around Alice to ooh and aah over the diamond.

Elaine gathered the dropped putters and carried them back to the counter. "Forget golf. We need to plan a wedding."

And that's when things got crazy.

Her friends showed up at her beach house with bridal magazines, and everyone had a different opinion about which style gown she should wear.

Alice had enough. She sneaked off to Manhattan, where an old friend with whom she had worked years ago in New York managed to arrange an appointment at Kleinfeld's, to buy an off-the-rack gown, meaning that Alice could take the dress with her rather than wait for it to be made and fitted. The next morning, Alice returned to Dewey with a floor-length, lace, sleeveless A-line wedding gown with a bateau neckline.

When the other Dewey Dames came to her house with more magazines and the promise that they'd narrowed down the search to a handful of choices, Alice greeted them in *her* gown. They were shocked, but all agreed she had chosen well, though they insisted they would have found one cheaper and prettier if she had just given them a little more time.

"And what will your bridesmaids be wearing?" Elaine asked.

Alice hadn't considered bridesmaids. But now she was faced with the possibility of disappointing the Dewey Dames. Without much thought, she answered, "Whatever you four can agree on."

Two days before the wedding, as Alice waited for Paul
to arrive to take her out to dinner, the other Dewey Dames
came to her condo. They were dressed in jeans and wearing black T-shirts with "Bridesmaid" written in white ink
across the chest; they were also wearing turquoise, plastic-bead necklaces. Alice knew that something was up.

"Tonight, we are having your bachelorette party," Elaine
announced.

Alice shook her head. "No. I can't do that. Paul is taking
me to dinner at some new restaurant he heard about."

Elaine handed her cell phone to Alice where there was
a text conversation to be read:

Elaine: *Surprise bachelorette party on Thursday. Don't
tell Alice, but keep her at home.*

Paul: *I don't think she wants a bachelorette party.*

Elaine: *Everybody should have one.*

Paul: *Okay. Just don't embarrass her.*

Elaine handed Alice a white T-shirt with "Bride to Be"
in black, the opposite of the bridesmaids' shirts, and led
her toward the bedroom while instructing the bride-to-be.
"Get in there and put on some jeans and this T-shirt. Don't
worry about a purse or anything else. All you need are
your house keys and your driver's license to prove you're
of legal drinking age. Ha-ha. And your health insurance
card—just in case."

Alice did as she was told, but first, while alone in her
room, she sent a quick text to Paul: *Bachelorette party.
Yikes. Follow me on* Find My Friends *in case I need to be*

rescued. Love you. She tucked her iPhone into her back pocket, hoping no one would notice it.

When Alice returned from her room, now dressed in accordance with the instructions given to her, her attire got more humiliating.

Sharon revealed a plastic crown with letters that spelled out "Bride." She pushed a button to make the letters light up and put it on Alice's head, making sure the plastic teeth of the crown were secured in her friend's hair. Then, she pinned a flashing "Here Comes the Bride" button on Alice's bridal T-shirt, while the other ladies placed additional plastic-bead necklaces around her neck.

Alice put Ginny in the guest bedroom where the litter box and a bowl of water were kept fresh each day for the kitten's easy access. She added a few toys before closing the door.

Outside the condo, there was a pink stretch limo, with tinted windows and an open moonroof. A man, dressed in linen slacks and a white shirt open at the neck in lieu of a tie, held the door open for the Dewey Dames.

As they climbed in, the ladies chatted over one another, all giving hints of the planned journey that they'd already arranged with the limo driver. "So, sit back, Alice, and enjoy the party," Margo said, handing her a glass of champagne.

The ladies clinked their plastic champagne flutes together. "Our first stops, of course, are bars here in Dewey," Elaine announced as they sipped their starting drinks.

At each of the establishments—Rusty Rudder, The Bottle and Cork, and The Starboard—they downed shooters with sexually evocative names like Buttery Nipple, Sex on the Beach, and Dirty Girl Scout Cookie. By the time they left Dewey, they were *feeling good*, as the expression goes.

On the way to Rehoboth, they heard a ding from Alice's pocket.

Elaine held out her hand, expecting Alice to give her the cell phone. "Why did you bring that with you?"

"I'm not answering it," she said, leaving the phone where it was. She was sure it was Paul checking up on her to see if she needed to be rescued yet. She was relieved he was following her on the app.

Margo passed around handfuls of the plastic-bead necklaces. "Time to play Mardi Gras." She stood up into the open moonroof and pulled Alice up next to her. Margo sang a song from *My Fair Lady* but paraphrased it to fit the wedding of Alice to Paul. "She's getting married Sunday morning …" She tossed necklaces toward the people who were walking down the sidewalk. "Come on, Alice, this is your job. We'll sing, and you throw."

The other ladies took turns popping up through the moonroof—like a Whac-a-Mole game—and singing, "She's getting married Sunday morning …"

The driver took the limo up and down Rehoboth Avenue twice before they ran out of necklaces to throw, at which time Elaine urged Alice to wave like Queen Elizabeth.

The limo pulled over to the Purple Parrot. "Look who's here!" Elaine shouted toward the open front of the bar, where a group of their other friends were seated and holding tables for them. A cheer broke out and the friends lifted their glasses. "To the bride!"

Inside the bar, Alice discovered that some of her Dewey neighbors were there, too, and had ordered trays of munchies for them. She crunched a corn chip filled with avocado but knew she should have something more substantial to eat, considering that she had not had dinner but had consumed more alcohol than she was accustomed to having.

While her friends were carrying on together, Alice wandered back to the restroom and typed a text for Paul: *drunnk hunggry want go home.* She clicked the send arrow and put the phone back into her pocket just before Connie came into the restroom.

"Are you okay?" she asked.

Alice leaned back against the wall. "Hungry and tired and drunk." Then her phone dinged. This time she checked it.

Paul had typed, *On my way.*

Connie read it and nodded. "Just try to stay with us for a little while so everyone will feel like they made your surprise party a success."

"Maybe if I eat something other than corn chips," she said.

Connie linked her arm with Alice's. "Let's get you a burger."

"Elaine told me not to bring any money."

"It's covered." Connie pulled out a wad of cash. "We made sure that each of us was prepared to pick up the tabs along the way. We had no idea that so many people in the bars would be treating all of us and not just the bride."

"You don't seem as wasted as I am," Alice said.

"Probably because I had a large dinner and because I have been cheating on the shooters, ordering the non-alcoholic ones. I'm the designated sober one for tonight's festivities."

Paul arrived and blended in with the rest of the partiers. He kept his arm around Alice, as she slowly picked at the hamburger and drank a ginger ale. When Alice finished most of the burger, Paul whispered something to Connie, then he took his bride-to-be's right hand and led her out of the bar.

Elaine spotted them and called out, "Hey, where are you two going?"

"For a romantic walk," Paul shouted back.

He led Alice to a bench on the boardwalk facing the sand dunes and ocean, which sparkled in the moonlight. With his arm around her shoulders, he kissed her temple. "I love you."

"I love you, too." She rested her head against him, closed her eyes, and started to doze.

In the background, the raucous sounds of the partiers filled the night air as the limo circled the gazebo at the end of Rehoboth Avenue. "Save it for the wedding night!" Elaine called out from the moonroof.

Alice opened her eyes. "Did I miss the limo? They'll wonder where I am."

"I told Connie that I would be taking you home tonight." He walked her to his car and drove her back to her Dewey condo. There, he made sure she got into her home safely and gave her a kiss at the door.

"Don't go, Paul."

He followed her into the condo, where they heard the kitten's sad meow of loneliness. "I'll get Ginny," he offered.

Alice stretched out on the sofa, a bit dizzy and exhausted. Paul sat on the floor by the kitty sack and played Catch the Feather, a stick with a feather at the end of its long cord that the kitten loved to bat with her paws. When Ginny was tired out, she went into her sleep sack.

Paul relaxed in the leather recliner but didn't fall asleep right away. Instead, he gazed at his soon-to-be wife and the kitten that would complete their little family.

Alice smiled at him and sang softly, "We're getting married Sunday morning …"

A Road Worth Taking

Zoe Burke drove her rental car, a nondescript, white Hyundai, up the crushed seashell driveway to the bright-yellow shingled cottage that belonged to her Aunt Tillie. After taking an American Airlines flight from Philadelphia to Salisbury, Maryland, and then driving to Chincoteague Island, Virginia, all she wanted was to unpack and take a long nap.

Just two days ago, she was presented with a challenging new project, one that could either advance her or get her fired from her position in the prestigious Dennison & Harmon Publishing Company. After seven years of being a successful copy editor, she had been thrilled when her boss, Larry Dennison, provided her the opportunity to prove herself as a developmental editor and move up in salary. It wasn't until she accepted the offer to work on the memoir *Philanthropy: One Humble Man's Journey* that she discovered the author was H. A. Kingston. His name had been bandied around the office, where he had a reputation as a bully, misogynist, and all-around asshole. Zoe's feelings of accomplishment crashed; she hadn't been awarded this position based on her copy-editing talents, but because all the other editors had been rejected by Kingston.

When her boss called her in to introduce her to the author, she was surprised that he didn't seem at all like the jerk she was expecting. Kingston was cordial, considerate, and quite handsome. Wavy, short, black hair; sharp, blue eyes behind Versace glasses; clean-shaven; and dressed in a beige summer suit. She was hopeful when he expressed his enthusiasm for this new partnership. But when he followed that with a litany of horrible experiences he had endured when working with "incompetent editors," she heard the subtext: *Watch out, or I'll throw you under the bus, too.* She noticed that her boss's lips tightened during this rant, yet he said nothing.

After his tirade, Kingston stood and smiled at her. "Here it is—my masterpiece." He handed her an oxblood leather portfolio and left the room.

Larry waited until the client was out of sight. "Open it."

When she opened the portfolio, she found a mess of papers, some typed and others handwritten on loose-leaf paper, with scratch-outs, renumbered pages, and penciled-in corrections. "How long do I have?"

"I told him two weeks … or a little more."

She stared down at the papers. "Two weeks?"

"You can work from home to avoid distractions. Believe me, you'll need quiet to plow through that garbage." Her boss popped one antacid and then a second. "Do the best you can to keep him, even if it means giving in sometimes. Silence and a smile can go a long way."

Silence and a smile? She needed time to think about the monumental task that loomed over her. With the manuscript in hand, she left the office early and walked home rather than take a bus, hoping the fresh air and exercise would calm her jagged nerves.

Two blocks from the brownstone apartment building where she lived, she saw flashing red lights and police barricades blocking the street and sidewalks ahead. *What in the world?* As she got closer, she saw that the building that had been next to hers was gone; all that was left was a pile of bricks and wood and pieces of furniture.

She showed a policeman her ID. "I live up there in apartment 3B."

"Not for the next few weeks. The building next to yours collapsed." He pointed to a short line of her neighbors. "Wait over there. We're taking one person at a time into the building to gather necessities. You'll need to find a temporary residence until your building is okayed for occupancy."

She noticed jagged cracks on the side of her building. Maybe she'd be needing a new apartment rather than a temporary place to live. And how? Affordable apartments were scarce.

She slept at a friend's place for two nights, but as Benjamin Franklin noted, "Guests, like fish, begin to smell after three days." Only family could be as forgiving. But with her parents living in California and her brother and his wife in Texas, the closest relative was her Aunt Tillie. Although her aunt's home was too far from Philadelphia for a commute, it was at least on the east coast and, after all, her boss had said that she could work from home. On Friday morning, Zoe phoned her aunt and explained the situation, asking if she could stay at her house.

"Of course you can stay here. And you'll have the whole house to yourself. The girls and I are leaving early tomorrow for a ten-day Caribbean cruise."

Zoe chuckled to herself. "The girls" were a group of senior citizens who were inseparable.

Tillie's house could be a solution, but Zoe thought it

would feel strange without her aunt there. She tried to backpedal, saying that she could find other arrangements, but her aunt insisted she come. "I'll leave a key for you with my next-door neighbor, Aidan. A nice young man. Around your age. And single, too."

Visiting Chincoteague just got more complicated. She feared her Aunt Tillie would try to play long-distance matchmaker.

＋

From the driver's seat of the rental car, Zoe scrutinized the neighbor's house. Dirty shingles that might have been white at some earlier time. Missing shutters, with one lying on the ground. A mismatch of black roof shingles, some dark, others faded. A front porch with bandaged screens.

She gingerly approached the dilapidated house and knocked on the front door several times, but no one answered. Only then did she notice furrows in the driveway that indicated a missing vehicle. *Great. A humid day and I'm stuck outside.* Her navy linen cropped pants were wrinkled from travel, and her sleeveless, white silk blouse was splotched with perspiration. She desperately needed to shower and change into something more appropriate. In the meantime, she'd have no choice but to wait outside until the neighbor's return.

She grabbed her copy of the *Philadelphia Business Journal* and walked to the back of her aunt's house, where she sat on the top step of the deck, surprised that her aunt's outdoor furniture was nowhere in sight. She was engrossed in an article about the current status of celebrity memoirs and didn't hear the pickup truck arrive, nor did she hear the squeak of her aunt's outdoor spigot. She only became aware of any of this when a wide spray of water splashed over the railing and drenched her.

Zoe screamed and jumped to her feet.

The water stopped, and a guy appeared at the bottom of the steps. "Are you okay?"

She brushed back her wet, shoulder-length, auburn hair and looked down at her saturated clothing, especially the silk blouse, through which her lace bra was now visible.

She saw his eyes quickly shift up to her face.

"Sorry. I didn't know anyone was back here. Hey, wait. You're Tillie's niece Zoe, aren't you?"

She guessed that he must be Aidan but was annoyed that he called her aunt by her first name. She felt a case of snippy come over her. "My mom is her niece. Technically, I'm her great niece."

"And technically, I'm her neighbor, Aidan." He gestured toward the not-so-white cottage. "Before your aunt left on her trip, she asked me to clean her siding and deck before you arrived," he said. "I guess I got the date wrong. I wasn't expecting you until tomorrow."

He looked as unkempt as the exterior of his house. Dirty, grayish-white T-shirt with the sleeves cut out, ripped jeans, wet tennis shoes. Tanned. "Live Life" tattooed on his shoulder.

"My aunt said you'd have the spare key to her cottage for me."

Aidan's eyebrows squinched together, and he shook his head. "She didn't tell me about that. Maybe she forgot that I gave her back the spare key after I resurfaced her living room floor."

No key. Yet another problem. *Is the universe so bored that it decided to see how much I can handle before I drop over?* Zoe exhaled her built-up frustration and texted her aunt, *Aiden says he doesn't have your key.* She stared at the phone, waiting for her aunt to text back.

"I doubt you'll get an immediate response. Tillie doesn't check her texts often."

Zoe started to wonder about her aunt's relationship with this guy. "How do you know?"

"Because it took an extra day to finish her floor while I waited for her to answer whether she wanted light or dark cherry stain." He checked his watch. "I'd like to get this deck cleaned and put her furniture back in place. So, while we're waiting for Tillie's response, why don't you sit on *my* deck and enjoy the shade for a while."

Aidan's backyard was a patchwork of uneven weeds and small plots of brown dirt that led to a prefabricated outbuilding secured by a heavy padlock. Judging from the sticker that still clung to the door, the shed was a recent purchase. At least something on his property was new.

His deck, which looked down over a wooded area, needed a cleaning more than her aunt's, and the siding on his house was mismatched and green with mildew. The deck furniture was littered with twigs and soiled with bird droppings. She sat on the edge of the cleanest cushion and stared down at her phone in anticipation of her aunt's response.

The ammonia smell of cat urine burned her nose, and a sudden movement from under her chair made her jump from the seat. "What—" A brown-and-black tabby with white paws emerged and disappeared down the steps. Zoe sighed. "Great. He has a cat." Then she heard a crash under the deck and walked down the steps to see what had happened, but there was so much junk stored under the deck—lawn equipment, crates, tires, beach chairs, an old screen door, and something wide covered by an extra-large brown tarp—she couldn't determine what had fallen.

Curiosity won. She peeked under the tarp and saw a wrought-iron outdoor table with four chairs and two chaise lounges, all with matching pink-and-rose-print vinyl cushions—her Aunt Tillie's favorite colors. She deduced that this was the missing deck furniture. She moved one of the chairs into the yard so she could sit on a clean surface.

Just then, her phone dinged with a new message.

Oops (emoji with round mouth). *Key on kitchen table. Forgot 2 give 2 him. Tell Aiden break back door.* Apparently, Aunt Tillie knew text slang.

Unlike her young-at-heart great aunt, Zoe could never use such shortcuts. As a copy editor, casual usage was unthinkable. So, Zoe typed back, *But with a broken door, your house won't be secure.*

The reply, *Course it will. My new door in his shed. Perfect time 2 replace. Gotta run. In port. Tour bus about 2 leave* (emoji wearing sunglasses).

When Aidan finished the pressure washing, Zoe shared her aunt's messages. He said, "That's just how Tillie is—so easy-going. Nothing ever bothers her."

She watched in shock as Aidan kicked down the old door. "Did you really need to literally *break* the door?"

"Why waste time with a tool when it's unnecessary?" He held out one of the hinges. It was rust-covered. "The hinges are crumbling, and the wood is rotted and can't be recycled. I'll be busting it up to cart it off anyway." He carried the pieces of the old door to his yard and returned with her aunt's newly purchased door, still in its box. "I see you found Tilley's cleaned furniture," he said.

Zoe couldn't read his tone. Was he accusing her of snooping under his deck, or was he just making an observation? "Is that a problem? I needed a place to sit, but your cat seems to have peed on your furniture."

"I don't have a cat."

"Well, I smelled cat on your deck. And then I saw it. A brown-and-black cat with white paws."

He shrugged. "Not mine. Probably one of the feral cats that live around here."

"If they're feral, why don't you do something to keep them away? I've read that mothballs repel cats."

He seemed surprised by her attitude. "The local rescue group has a better way to deal with the feral population. Trap. Neuter. Return. Stopping the feral cats from breeding is a humane way to decrease that population. In the meantime, many townies supply dry cat food and fresh water to keep the cats from starving or dying in the summer heat." He slit open the box and removed the installation directions.

Zoe felt a smirk spread on her face. "And, in return, the cats pee on your deck and possessions."

Her expression was wasted on him, as he didn't look up from the installation materials. "You either love animals or you don't."

She heard the unmasked accusation in his tone. "It seems counterintuitive to release them rather than put them up for adoption."

"Stray cats are adoptable; feral cats are not, except for kittens that are young enough to be socialized." He removed a layer of white Styrofoam, revealing a ruby-red, split door, like a stable door, but with a circular window at eye level.

"Did my aunt approve this? It's not even wood, is it?"

He lifted the door from the box with some difficulty and walked it over to the exterior wall of the house. "It was a compromise. I suggested she get a composite door that will hold up better in salt air and that has a steel interior for security. She insisted she didn't need a security door for her deck, but when I showed her the style choices from this manufacturer, she fell in love with the stable-door design. Fait accompli."

French. As though I wouldn't know what he was saying. Zoey responded, "Oui, done deal." She watched for his reaction, but Aidan kept a straight face.

He tossed her two keys held together with a thin ring of silver wire. "These are the keys to Tillie's new back door. Try not to lose them."

Zoe entered the house and saw the forgotten house key on the kitchen table, attached to a lanyard made of braided leather in ocean shades of blues and greens, draped across a framed photo of Zoe at her graduation from the University of Maryland, College Park. That was over six years ago. There was also a sticky note, on which her aunt had written in her beautiful cursive penmanship, "This is my Zoe, my precious niece, the one I told you about. Keep an eye on her while I'm away."

No, thank you, Aunt Tillie. I'll be fine without him.

Zoe added one of the backdoor keys to the lanyard and put the extra key on a hook above the faucet. She returned

the photo to the fireplace mantel in the living room and
started to crumple the note. But she stopped. She smoothed
the paper, folded it into a smaller square, and placed it in
her wallet behind a photo that was taken of her with Aunt
Tillie during a family Thanksgiving holiday when Zoe
was still in high school. *Note to self: When Aunt Tillie gets
home, we must do a selfie together.*

After a quick shower accompanied by the not-so-sweet
music of the backdoor installation, Zoe donned more appropriate summer clothing—shorts and a tank top—and
went to the kitchen to raid the fridge and begin her editing
work. Aunt Tillie had made several gallons of sweet tea,
her favorite homemade beverage, and had stocked up on
frozen dinners and luncheon meats, items she knew Zoe
would enjoy. On the counter, there was a large basket filled
with homemade sweets—oatmeal cookies and sea-foam
candy—as well as salty snacks.

She poured a tall glass of iced tea and put three oatmeal
cookies on one of her aunt's pink ceramic dessert dishes.
Then, she opened Kingston's portfolio. Staring down at the
uneven pile of papers made her stomach do a one-eighty.
*Face it. I can't get out of this. No matter how difficult it
may be, this is my opportunity to demonstrate my worth
to Dennison & Harmon.*

With red pen poised, she began reading the opening
chapter, "Taking the First Step." Clichéd boring title.
Complex sentences that lost the reader in a jumble of
superlative adjectives. But she held back her immediate
instincts to make the page bleed—a favorite expression of

her writing professors—and tried to focus on the overall content, empty as that might be. The chapter was nothing more than a self-congratulatory homage from the author to himself.

Sentence by sentence, she jotted down corrections and suggestions, then erased them again. How far dare she push this author who had already dumped more experienced editors? "Silence and a smile," she muttered.

Midway through the last cookie, her phone rang. Larry Dennison's office number flashed on the screen.

"I need you in the office tomorrow morning," he said.

Crap. She had forgotten to tell him about her temporary move. "Larry, did you see the news on Wednesday?"

"Is this really important?" he asked.

"Yes. There was a building collapse, and both neighboring apartment buildings were shut down for inspection. My apartment was in one of them. Consequently, I needed to make a temporary move, which seemed fine since you said I could work from home for the next few weeks, so I left Philly."

"And where are you now?" He sounded annoyed.

She tried to say it with as little emotion as possible, like reciting an alphabet or saying "God bless you" to a sneeze. "I'm staying with my aunt in Virginia."

"Virginia?" His voice jumped an octave. "Kingston is coming to Philadelphia tomorrow and wants to meet with both of us."

Her dreams of leaving the cubicles of copy editors and proofreaders and having a private office on the editors' floor of the publishing house was hanging in the balance. "We can do a virtual conference through GoToMeeting," she suggested.

He seemed calmer at this recommendation. "It's unusual, of course, but I know that a few of our editors have used that method to speak with clients. I'm willing to try, but let's practice with it first. Send me a link and put me on speaker phone to talk me through it. I don't want anything to go wrong. Kingston is a pain in my … never mind. But he's a cash cow, so we need to keep him in this contract."

Zoe opened her laptop and clicked on the GoToMeeting bookmark. "No Internet connection" flashed on her screen. She searched for nearby networks. Several were listed, and one had a robust signal, but that network—beach#sun#1—was locked. She sighed.

"What's happening?" her boss asked. "I don't see anything on my end."

"Internet issue."

His voice jumped again. "No, no, no. We can't have this. You need to find reliable Wi-Fi in that town. Check the library, or a coffee shop, or even a hotel. Surely someone has high-speed access."

"I can use my cell-phone app."

"No. Cell-phone towers can be less dependable than Wi-Fi. And what if we need to share documents on the screen? You can't do that very well on a phone." He got quiet for a moment, and then said, "I'll tell Kingston we need to postpone the meeting for forty-eight hours; that should give you enough time to fix this problem. If you can't find a high-speed Wi-Fi connection for your laptop by tomorrow, then you best be on your way back to Philadelphia. Got it?" He didn't stay on the line for her answer.

Zoe slammed her laptop shut, tossed it into her computer

bag, jumped in the car, and used the vehicle GPS to find the closest library.

As she drove down streets of historic-looking buildings, her GPS announced, "arriving at destination," but she didn't believe it. The white building looked like a storefront. Yet, sure enough, a sign said "Chincoteague Island Library." The inside of the library, with its balconied second floor of shelved books, seemed like a Hollywood set for a nineteenth-century storyline. She felt her jaw drop in awe, a reaction that caught the attention of a friendly librarian. "Good afternoon. May I assist you?"

"I'm hoping the library has Wi-Fi."

He smiled. "We do. Free Wi-Fi."

The right answer. In her mind, she was crossing her fingers in preparation for her next question. "In two days, I have a very important virtual meeting with my boss and a client. Is there a private room where I could have a GoToMeeting conference? It will involve my having the sound turned up for a three-way discussion."

She read his face before he answered, "I'm sorry. We don't have any private rooms, but—"

"Well, thanks anyway." Zoe didn't mean to cut him off; it was just that she was desperate to find a solution that didn't involve returning to Philly. And if the library couldn't help, she needed to find another option.

"Wait. Our Wi-Fi signal is strong and can be accessed outside the library in the waterfront park. If the weather is fine, which our local weatherman has promised, you can have your virtual conference while sitting at a picnic table under cover, looking out at the water. Just follow the brick walkway toward the channel; you can't miss the blue tin roof."

She almost hugged him. "Wonderful! Thank you. I so appreciate your help."

✦

With her problem solved, Zoe—exhausted from the travel and the stress her boss placed on her—decided to take some free time to wander around downtown. At the end of the block, she found Sundial Books. It had been so long since she'd taken the time to read a book for pleasure rather than as copy-edit work.

Just like her experience at the library, she was immediately greeted and felt welcome here, too.

"I need a book," she said. Then, realizing how stupid that statement was, she broke into laughter. "Duh. Of course. Why else would I enter a bookstore?"

The woman behind the counter smiled at her. "Well, some people wander into the store looking for postcards, local art, or Chincoteague gifts."

"What I really need is a romance novel. An escape from the pressure of my job."

"A beach read?" the woman asked. "I have an excellent suggestion." She led Zoe to a shelf of regional authors and handed her *Island of Miracles* by Amy Schisler. "The writer lives on the Eastern Shore of Maryland, and the story takes place here on Chincoteague Island."

Zoe glanced at the back cover. The pitch identified the protagonist as someone whose "world comes crashing down." It made Zoe think of the building in Philadelphia that came crashing down, and the chance that her new position at the publishing house would likewise fall. "It seems a perfect match for me." She purchased the book and stepped outside.

On the other side of Main Street, Zoe was intrigued by a building called the Antique Mall, where several small shops were housed. Inside the mall, she saw a woman seated at a table in the corridor between the first-floor shops. On the table was a cage containing a small calico cat that had a bandage on the top of one of its ears. Zoe glanced at the pamphlet the woman held out. "No, thank you. I'm not a cat person."

"Perhaps you can pass it along to someone who might be able to help us with the Trap-Neuter-Return program." It was the expression Aidan had used. She wondered about Aunt Tilly's opinion of this approach.

Just then, a little girl, four years old at the most, with blonde braids, rushed past her to get a better look at the cat.

"Mommy! Mommy! A kitty!" The child pointed to the cat's ear. "The kitty has a boo-boo."

Zoe listened as the woman explained that the cat's ear had been clipped to let everyone know that the cat had been ... fixed, made better. She avoided using "spayed" or "neutered," as the child was too young to understand.

"What's the kitty's name?" the girl asked.

"She doesn't have a name. What do you think her name should be?" the woman asked.

"Peaches," she answered.

Her mom laughed. "It's her favorite fruit." Then, "Come on, Becca. Your grandpop has been waiting on that bench outside long enough."

Zoe watched them leave the building. She thought of

what Aidan had said and wondered at the answer. *Am I the kind of person who doesn't love animals? Or was I just in a crappy mood this morning and took it out on him?*

When she got to her aunt's house and opened the front door, the troublesome manuscript with its uneven pages was waiting on the table, reminding her of the difficult job she faced. "Later," she said aloud. She pushed it aside to have room to make a sandwich, but apparently, she hadn't created enough space, because a splatter of mayonnaise landed on the title page. Under normal circumstances, she would have freaked out at damaging an author's manuscript, but today she grinned as she dabbed the blot of oily mayo with a paper towel. "Take that, Kingston, you conceited moron!"

She retreated to the outdoor deck with the romance novel and was pleasantly surprised at the change in Aunt Tillie's deck. Not only was the surface clean but also her aunt's outdoor furniture had been returned, including a pink-and-white striped umbrella that Zoe hadn't seen earlier. She settled on one of the chaise lounges and opened her book.

After a day spent reading rather than editing, she locked the doors, opened the bedroom window to let the cool evening air fill the room, rolled down the old-fashioned, white chenille bedspread, and fell asleep. She dreamed of lying in a hammock at her parents' house and listening to her mom playing the piano in the background. Soothing.

At four in the morning, a loud screeching sound woke her. She held her breath and listened for a repeat of the noise. Had she been dreaming, or was the sound real? She turned on the porch lights and saw two small animals, one chasing the other toward the wooded area behind the house. *Cats!*

Zoe tried to return to her pleasant dream, but it seemed she would never get back to sleep. She tossed and turned until the sun streaming in through the sheer curtains of the guest room announced daybreak. Groggy from so little sleep, she made chamomile tea, hung two of her aunt's beach towels over the curtain rod to block the sun, stretched out across the bed fully clothed, and finally nodded off—until a continuous, loud, high-pitched whine shook her awake. It was the sound of a circular saw cutting through wood.

She didn't need to look out a window to know it was Aidan. She ran out on the deck and shouted at him, but his back was turned, and he couldn't hear her above the noise of the saw.

Zoe rushed down the steps and toward him. "Hey!"

She didn't know whether he had heard her shout or had stopped because he was at the bottom of the wood panel, but he turned to face her with a tight-lipped smile. "Good morning, Zoe. Beautiful day, isn't it?"

His eye-protection goggles made him look like a mad scientist, but she wasn't in a laughing mood. "Aren't there any HOA rules about noise levels in the morning?"

He appeared surprised by her question. "First of all, there isn't an HOA in this neighborhood, and second, it's noon."

Noon?

They stared at one another, each waiting for the other to respond.

Finally, Aidan said, "I'm sorry if the noise is bothering you, but this is the only time I have to work on my own house. The rest of the week is scheduled for my handyman services." His tone made clear that he was aggravated more than apologetic. "All this would have been done yesterday if I hadn't had to clean Tillie's deck so that her inconsiderate, self-absorbed niece would have a nice outdoor space to enjoy."

Hearing her aunt's name hit home and made his insults ring true. Her outrage turned to embarrassment. Aunt Tillie had probably described her as a wonderful person—certainly not the shrew she'd been with Aidan. But she couldn't bring herself to say she was sorry. Instead, she asked, "Is it really noon?"

A car pulled up between the houses, and a woman's voice called out, "Yoo-hoo, Aidan!" A petite, silver-haired woman, dressed in denim cropped pants and a "Margaritas Made Me Do It" T-shirt, was hobbling down the driveway, with her left foot in a boot cast. Despite the unevenness of her walk, she was carrying a covered dish. "You must be Tillie's great niece, Zoe. I'm Lorraine, one of your aunt's posse. I just love that word." She giggled. "I was supposed to go on the cruise with the girls, too, but," she pointed to her foot, "my surgeon nixed that idea. Anyway, Tillie told me to keep an eye out for you."

"Thank you," Zoe said, wondering what Lorraine had brought her.

But the woman handed the covered dish to Aidan. "I made you some dumplings with gravy."

Aidan held the dish in one hand while hugging her with the other arm. "You're so sweet."

A blush come over the woman's face. "It's the least I can do for all that time you spent fixing my ceiling fan," she said.

Then, she took a folded sheet of yellow notepaper from

her pocket and gave it to Zoe. "Keep this with you in your purse. If you need anything at all while Tillie is on the cruise, call or text me."

Lorraine gave Aidan another hug and hobbled back the way she came.

He watched the elderly woman until she safely reached her car. "Your Aunt Tillie's friends are such good people," he said.

✦

Zoe returned to her aunt's living room, but napping was no longer an option. She was fully awake and energized. She knew that she should work on Kingston's manuscript, but her questions about Aidan were heavy on her mind. She called her aunt's cell phone. "Aunt Tillie?"

"Is everything okay?" her aunt asked.

"Of course. I wanted to let you know that your friend Lorraine stopped by."

"And?"

"That's all."

Her aunt tsk-tsked. "Zoe, what's the real reason for your call?"

"What do you know about your neighbor Aidan?"

"And you are asking this why?"

"Lorraine brought him food, and he called her 'sweet' and hugged her."

"So?"

"Well, don't you think it's a little weird for a young guy to flirt with a senior citizen?"

Her aunt laughed. "Zoe, if you think a hug between friends is flirting, then you need to get out more. Unless he dipped her and they French-kissed, that hug was a friendly gesture and nothing more."

Zoe felt foolish, but she couldn't let it go. "How does he act around you, Aunt Tillie?"

"As though I were his great-aunt," she answered. "He goes out of his way to help me and all his neighbors. Most of us are up in age, and he's young, strong, and capable of fixing things for us, which he does as a kindness. He won't accept more than the cost of materials. That's why Lorraine brought him a homemade something-or-other. We all do that," she said. "And it won't surprise you that he loves my crab cakes."

Zoe wanted to feel reassured but having lived in an urban area, she had a strong sense of distrust. "But, Aunt Tillie, what do you *really* know about him? How long has he lived next door to you? Why did he move to the island?"

"You sound like a reporter," she said. "Here's what I know to be true. Aidan bought that house two months ago and has been fixing it up bit by bit. He's a good neighbor and a kind person. The first time I met him, he saw me struggling to carry an old bookcase to the edge of the road to be picked up by Habitat ReStore. He not only carried it for me but also fixed one of the shelves and filled in a gash with wood putty. The case looked so good that I almost decided to keep it, but someone else probably needed it more," she said. "Anyway, I told all my friends at the senior center about him, so you could say it's my fault that he's become a busy handyman."

"And that's all you know?"

"Zoe, dear, I've been on this earth long enough to trust my gut. But if knowing his life story will make you feel better, invite him over for a glass of wine so you can get acquainted with one another. Who knows, you might have something in common," her aunt said. "Oops! Gotta go now; the girls are waiting for me. We have some serious shopping to do at the straw market."

"I love you, Aunt Tillie."

"I love you, too."

She considered her Aunt Tillie to be a *wise sage*, an expression her aunt would point out as redundant and for which Zoe would suggest the literary term *tautology*, elevating her word choice as intentional. Regardless, Zoe dreaded facing Aidan after their previous confrontations.

The shed door was locked, and Aidan was not in sight, but the presence of his truck in the driveway assured Zoe he was home. She ascended the deck and saw that the backdoor was open with only the screen door closed. She knocked. "Aidan?"

No one came to the door, so she leaned her face against the screen to peek inside. What she saw astonished her. The kitchen was not what she expected to see in this old cottage, especially as rundown as its exterior was. The room looked more like a Manhattan condo pictured in *The New York Times*: clean lines, upscale cabinets, a huge island with hanging wood rack for storing glassware, refinished wood flooring, a restored farmhouse table with six chairs, and a clear view of an open-concept living area with a spiral staircase leading up to the second floor.

While her face was still pressed against the screen, she saw Aidan walking toward the kitchen with only a white towel wrapped around him. Quickly, she turned and started toward the steps.

"Zoe?" his voice called from inside the house.

She froze in her tracks. "Hi, Aidan. I wanted to ask you something, but it can wait."

He opened the screen door for her. "Come on in."

"I can come back later."

He looked down at the towel, then up at her. "Here's an idea. I'll go back upstairs and get dressed. In the meantime, help yourself to some sweet tea in the fridge."

"Sweet tea?" she asked.

"Yeah, Tillie makes the best sweet tea I've ever had."

Zoe's guard went up again. "My aunt makes you sweet tea?"

He held up his hands in surrender. "Not any more. When I first moved in, she brought me a jug of her tea as a welcome-to-the-neighborhood gift, and she gave me her recipe." He handed her a tall glass from the rack. "I promise that mine is exactly like Tillie's. Now, if you'll excuse me, I'll exchange this towel for some shorts and a shirt." He disappeared up the spiral staircase.

Zoe opened the fridge and saw the iced tea in an antique Virginia Dairy bottle. She filled her glass but continued to stare into the open fridge. She couldn't help but take stock of the other items because she believed that what people consume says a lot about them. Skim milk, orange juice, two bottles of chardonnay, a slice of blueberry pie, horseradish mustard and some less interesting condiments, bowls of cherries and of black grapes, half of a watermelon, canisters of potato salad and cucumber salad, wedges of various cheeses, Lorraine's covered dish, and Kerrygold

Irish butter. He ate well. That was something in his favor. But she still wasn't sure she trusted him.

Her phone rang. Unknown caller, but the area code was 212. New York City. Was Kingston trying to reach her without her boss present? She set the phone on "Do Not Disturb."

Zoe closed the fridge door and was sitting at the kitchen island when she heard Aidan come down the stairs. He had changed into olive cargo shorts and a white, New York City Marathon T-shirt.

"How's the tea?" he asked.

"Just like Aunt Tillie's."

He poured a glass of tea for himself and joined her at the island. "So, what did you want to ask me?"

"I ..." she began. "First, I need to apologize for being so ... irritable yesterday and this morning."

"Irritable? I hadn't noticed." He couldn't stop his grin. "Truthfully, I could have reacted better, too." He sipped his iced tea. "Your aunt says you're from Philadelphia. And an editor?"

"Mostly a copy editor." Zoe didn't want to talk about herself. Her whole reason for coming over to Aidan's house was to find out about him. "And you? Where did you live before moving to Chincoteague?"

"New York."

"Manhattan?"

"I worked downtown, but I lived in Queens."

Zoe jumped in with the big question. "Where did you work?"

He laughed. "I already told you. Manhattan."

"I meant, what did you do as a job in New York?"

He paused as though weighing his answer. "I was a suit."

She sighed. Was he purposely evading the question, or just playing coy? "What kind of suit?" she asked.

He thought some more. "A stuffy suit. A navy-blue suit. An expensive suit. A suit that someone in the Village has bought by now at a ridiculously low price. Certainly, they'll value it more than I did." He leaned his chin on his hand, with laughter in his eyes.

This was going to be more difficult than she had expected. Yet, rather than feeling impatience at his enigmatic answers, she felt a sudden attraction to him. She could understand now how Aidan had won over his aunt and her friends. He was charming.

Zoe's fitbit vibrated. "A text from my boss." *Call me ASAP*. "Oh crap. I forgot to take my phone off the 'Do Not Disturb.' I'd better take care of this."

He held the door open for her. "But then we'll continue our conversation, right? It'll be *my* turn to ask the questions, you know."

"Sure," she answered, but wondered, *About what?*

"I'll gather some snacks for us and meet you on Tillie's deck," he said.

She gave a thumbs-up and dialed while walking to her aunt's house. "Larry, I'm so sorry I missed your call."

"Did you arrange Wi-Fi for tomorrow's conference?" he asked.

"Yes. It's all worked out."

"Is it a safe connection?"

She doubted that free Wi-Fi was secure, but she answered, "Of course. And I'll be where no one can overhear our conversation." At least, she hoped for privacy at Waterfront Park, and not a noisy family with children eating lunch nearby.

"How much have you accomplished?"

She opened the door to her aunt's kitchen where the manuscript rested on the table. "A good start, but it's difficult to do my job and yet find ways to appease the author. For a lawyer, his writing is horrible."

"I know, but I'm counting on you to find the compromises." He put on his cheerleader voice. "I've seen you handle prima donnas before. Remember, you got Kaylyn Smithe's third gothic mystery to print in record time. And, better yet, she demanded you be given her fourth book when it's ready for editing. If you can get Kingston to print, I promise you a large bonus."

"I'll need it for ulcer surgery or time in a psych hospital."

Larry chuckled. "Just identify some good stuff in the manuscript to compliment during tomorrow's conference."

"I'll do my best."

Aidan appeared outside the screen door. "Food delivery!" He carried a large thermal bag to the wrought-iron table.

Zoe joined him and helped arrange the goodies: A basket of crackers, a plastic tub of seedless grapes, cheese wedges, a bottle of chilled chardonnay, and two wine glasses.

Aidan poured the wine. "Did everything turn out okay with your boss?"

"Mostly. But I'm supposed to list some nice things to say to the author tomorrow about his manuscript."

"Bad writing? Or nasty author?" he asked.

"Both." She nibbled on a piece of brie. "I wish I could

get out of this editing assignment."

"Why can't you?"

"My boss promoted me specifically for this project, and he's offered a substantial bonus if I succeed."

"But is it worth the trouble?"

She shrugged. "I guess. Who wouldn't want to move up in position and make a great salary? And if I can get Kingston's book into shape, then …." She stopped when she noticed that Aidan's face paled as though he'd seen a ghost.

"Kingston?" he asked.

"Yeah. Hamilton Alexander Kingston. Have you heard of him?"

"You could say that," he said. "I was on my way up the ladder in his law firm."

Zoe felt her mouth drop open in surprise. Aidan was a lawyer.

"And no, I wasn't fired. I quit."

"May I ask why you quit?"

Aidan answered with his own question. "What do you already know about Hamilton Kingston?"

Zoe crossed her arms. "That he's a narcissistic jerk who is self-absorbed and self-serving. And I have to pretend to like his book and, figuratively, kiss his ass as much as possible as I try to edit his manuscript, so my publisher isn't embarrassed when the book appears in print."

"You mean, *Philanthropy—One Humble Man's Journey*?" he asked, assuming a stuffy intonation.

She was surprised he knew about the book. "That's the one."

"He bragged about it constantly. But the title alone was enough for me to figure it was nonsense. He wouldn't know 'humble' if it smacked him in the face. And any act of philanthropy he ever did was for tax write-offs, free advertising, or as a way to distract people from the fact that he defends big pharma companies against complaints by patients whose lives were ruined by medicines that didn't do what they promised."

"Is that why you quit?"

He nodded. "When I was named junior partner, I moved from minor cases to big-buck cases. I was part of the team that represented New Way Inventions Pharmaceuticals in Village Women's Oncology v. NWIP. It was my opportunity to appear in court with Kingston. In terms of status at the law firm, this was a big deal."

Zoe recalled the story. It had been first-page news throughout the spring. "The company that promised a less expensive medical treatment for ovarian cancer?"

His eyes focused on the ice cubes in his glass. "In actuality, all it did was mask the spread of the cancer and prolong life until no other treatment was effective. The original formula did pass the tests, but the cheaper version's lack of success was kept hidden as NWIP continued to rework the formula. Basically, wealthy patients received the original formula while Medicaid patients received the one that was still being developed. When called out for this unethical behavior, the company made the patients look like fools for not reading the fine print."

Zoe shook her head. "And NWIP won."

"Yes." He looked up from his glass. "I watched fragile ex-patients, wearing bandanas to cover their bald heads, shout and cry when the verdict was read. Kingston, his eyes bright with victory, stood to shake the hand of the CEO of

NWIP. It was disgusting. When he turned to congratulate me, I turned my back on him and walked out. While Kingston was enjoying a celebration dinner with his clients, I returned to my office and wrote a letter of resignation. The next day, I left the city, not sure where I was going, just knowing that I needed to find a new path, one that I could live with. And that's how I landed on Chincoteague Island."

Zoe thought about the magnitude of Aidan's choice to walk away from such a prestigious law firm. "My Kingston troubles seem minor in comparison. My boss just expects me to mask my feelings about the book by following his personal platitude: 'Silence and a smile can go a long way.' On the other hand, you gave up a partnership rather than act against your morals."

"It's apples and oranges. I quit because my boss was amoral, but I didn't know that until I saw his disgusting behavior at the conclusion of the case against women whose lives were sacrificed in the name of corporate profit." Aidan opened the tub of grapes and offered them to Zoe. "In your case, you're the sacrificial lamb put on the pyre by your boss."

She took a few grapes. "But Larry's a good guy. He's just doing what's best for the company."

"The same thing can be said about the CEO of that pharmaceutical company. But success should not be dependent on using others. Sure, Kington's book will sell, but how will you feel about having your name attached to a book on which you compromised?"

Zoe knew in her heart Aidan was right. She munched the grapes one by one, quietly considering his question.

"Maybe you could ask that the manuscript be given to someone else," he suggested.

"Kingston already rejected everyone else on the editing staff. That's why I got promoted. He would balk at having someone from the copy-edit department suggest changes in the manuscript, so Larry moved me up to the fourth floor and gave me an office—small, but still an office of my own."

Aidan shook his head. "And if you tell the truth to Kingston, he'll dump you, too, and you'll be back to copy editing?"

"Maybe not. As long as it's Kingston doing the dumping and not my boss, I'll still have my new position." She realized how stupid that sounded. "Crap! I guess I'm as self-serving as Kingston."

Aidan smiled at her. "No, you're not. Kingston is a top dog in his field. He could run naked down Fifth Avenue and not lose a client. If anything, it would be front-page news and he'd love that. On the other hand, you're a working woman who needs to stay employed."

Aunt Tillie was right about Aidan being a good guy. "Thanks for putting it into perspective and providing food for thought—literally as well as figuratively."

Aidan held up his wine glass and offered a toast. "To finding our way!"

"To finding the *right* way," she corrected.

They both took deep sips of the chilled wine.

Then, Aidan added, "Ah, but is there only one right way?" He tossed a grape at her.

She tossed it back. "I guess not. But you have the advantage of a profession that is needed everywhere. You could start your own law practice here on the island."

He rolled the grape between his fingers. "I've thought about it. But, no. I'm happiest working with my hands. And I like helping people. Although I'd consider doing pro bono for the Legal Aid Bureau." He tossed the grape off the deck. "How about you? If you stopped working for a publishing house, how else might you use your skills and talents?"

"And make money? There's the problem." She sipped her wine, enjoying the slight buzz it gave her. "I could work for a local newspaper. Or use my minor in library science, but I don't think the island library needs extra staff."

"Maybe they do. Don't close a door in your own face." He refilled their wine glasses. "What is your dream job? The career to fulfill you for the rest of your life?"

She closed her eyes, but she knew the answer. She just hesitated to share it aloud. "I've always wanted to start my own small publishing house."

When she opened her eyes, Aidan's face was bright with enthusiasm. "That's it. That's the one that comes from your heart. Write it down and keep it in front of you during your meeting with Kingston and your boss. If you can't do the editing of that book while satisfying your own standards, you should walk away. Remember that you have a better career waiting for you."

"And how will I pay my rent in Philly? That is, if my apartment building is still standing." She saw he was about to ask what she meant, but she stopped him. "It's a long story and not useful at this moment."

"You should pack up your stuff, leave Philadelphia, and move here with your aunt. Despite her active lifestyle, she's getting up in age and, although it's none of my business, I'd feel better if Tillie had a roommate."

Zoe felt as though a lightbulb had flashed in her mind. His idea was viable: She knew how to build a website. She would arrange to have Wi-Fi at her aunt's house. And she could seek the help of the staffs at Sundial Books and the Island Library; they'd know how to contact local authors and how she might get the word out that self-publishing was no longer the only option. "I'll think about it. A lot will depend on how tomorrow's virtual conference goes."

"Virtual conference? But Tillie doesn't have Wi-Fi," he said.

"Yes, I know. And if I pursue my dream job, I'll rectify that. In the meantime, I'm going to the Waterfront Park in the morning to use the library's connection."

He grinned. "I have a better idea. You can use my Wi-Fi."

"Are you beach#sun#1?" she asked. "It came up on my laptop, but it's password protected."

"It's an easy password." He pushed up his sleeve to reveal the tattoo Zoe had noticed at their first meeting: "Live Life."

Although the park was a good choice, staying here was better. No problems with outdoor noise. No worry about a passing shower. And, most importantly, no misinterpretation of why she was sitting outdoors by the water as though on vacation. "Thanks."

The bottle of wine was empty, and the cheese was suffering from the mid-day heat. "We should move this into the house before it becomes garbage."

They carried everything into Aunt Tillie's kitchen, but the dreaded manuscript was still on the table. "Damn it," Zoe said. "A reminder that I have to come up with some nice things to say to Kingston tomorrow." She looked to Aidan, hoping he'd talk her into dumping the papers onto the floor and continuing their conversation instead of her worrying over her job.

But he didn't do that. "How about I give you three hours to work? At five o'clock, I'll prepare dinner at my house and then come back over here to save you from the dreaded monster's gobbledygook."

✦

Zoe searched page after page, looking for anything positive to say that would not be a complete lie. She made a list of page numbers and safe comments, but for every positive note, there was an equal criticism. "Good control of adjectives, but superlatives are overused." "Good sentence variety, but fragments should be avoided." "Good vocabulary, but the writer needs to avoid repetition of such words within a single paragraph." She started to write, "A bit too much ego jumping from the pages," but crossed it out. There was no way she could say that and remain employed at Dennison & Harmon Publishing.

She was frustrated and scared of what might happen during the virtual conference tomorrow. Could she convincingly pretend to like Kingston's manuscript, or would she fail miserably? Would she lose her job? Or would she quit?

She had another fifteen minutes before Aidan returned. She stepped outside and discovered that a cool breeze had returned to the deck. She lay back on a chaise lounge and stared up at the azure sky. *This is heavenly. I could definitely live here for the rest of my life.*

A tiny mew, followed by another, came from somewhere below. Zoe descended the stairs from the deck and followed the sound.

Her aunt's deck was lower than Aidan's, so there wasn't room for much storage underneath. The mewing was coming from behind a section of deck skirting that had pulled loose.

She knelt on the grass and looked through the gap. There she saw a large, black cat lying beside three newborn kittens. The mother cat stared at her and made a soft hissing sound, so Zoe backed away.

At that moment, Aidan approached. "Planning to play hide and seek?" he asked.

"There's a feral cat and babies under Aunt Tillie's deck."

Aidan gave a questioning look. "I doubt it's a feral cat. They prefer living in colonies away from human contact." He looked under the deck and called, "Here, kitty-kitty."

In a moment, the black cat came out and jumped into his arms. "This is Cloud," he said, pointing to the white patch of fur on the cat's forehead. "When I first saw her last month, I thought she was a feral cat, too. But she was too comfortable with humans. I assumed she was somebody's pet, but when she kept showing up and sitting on the deck steps while I worked, I figured she was neither feral nor a house cat."

"She's a stray?" Zoe asked.

"More likely what they call a free-ranger. She wanders around the neighborhood, eats whatever people offer her, and sleeps wherever she wants. She loves your aunt. Tillie usually puts out a dish of cat food and a bowl of water, which is probably why Cloud decided to give birth here."

The cat jumped down and returned to her kittens. Together they watched the momma cat fuss over her babies.

"So cute," Zoe said.

"They say all babies are cute, don't they? I'll be right back."

Zoe enjoyed watching the newborn kittens climb over one another to be closest to their mother. Even though she'd never been drawn to cats before, she wished she could reach in and hold the kittens.

When Aidan returned, he was carrying a cardboard box that had been cut partway down. Inside, there was a plush towel. "Zoe, would you check under Tillie's kitchen sink. I think that's where she keeps the cat food."

Sure enough, Zoe found the bag of dry kibble and brought it to Aidan.

He pulled the skirting section back farther, scattered some food on the grass a few feet away, and the cat re-emerged to eat.

Aiden crawled under the deck and brought the first kitten out. He placed it in the box. The mother cat rushed over, looked into the box, and seemed content, but stayed nearby and watched as he placed the next two kittens in the box.

When he lifted the box and walked toward his deck, both Zoe and Cloud followed along. He opened the door to his house and let the cat follow him inside, where he placed the box in the corner of the kitchen and put a bowl of water on the floor.

Cloud lapped some water and then jumped into the box with her babies and allowed them to nurse.

"Now what?" Zoe asked.

He nodded toward the plates of food on his farmhouse table. "We eat our sandwiches."

"I mean, what happens to Cloud and the kittens?"

"I'll keep them here tonight and take them to the vet tomorrow morning for a checkup and to schedule a spaying for Cloud after her babies are weaned. Getting them and myself out of the house will also eliminate distractions during your virtual meeting. But for now, let's eat."

After finishing some delicious seafood wraps and cucumber salad, Aidan and Zoe walked back to Tillie's house. When Zoe paused at the door and looked up into his dark-brown eyes, Aiden kissed her. "Good night, Zoe. See you in the morning."

Long into the night, she thought of his kiss. She thought of how difficult returning to Philadelphia would be now that she had found someone special. *Yes, Aunt Tillie, you were right. He's a keeper.* She imagined living here with Aidan, both of them on similar journeys to find a future worth having and jobs that would fit into each other's lives. And how nice it would be to live by the ocean and work from home or in a cute little office along Main Street and never ride a bus to a skyscraper ever again. But, more importantly, how great it would be to wake up each morning next to the love of her life.

What am I? A romantic teenager? I've only known him for two days. And the kiss? Maybe when I looked into his eyes tonight, he assumed I expected one. And starting my own business? A small publishing house? The cost? The details? And why bother when I already work for a nationally respected publisher? It was only a silly daydream.

The next morning, Aidan cleared his table and set up Zoe's laptop so the background for her virtual meeting would be closed plantation shutters, the best version of a business office he could provide. He stood behind her while she connected to his Wi-Fi.

"If you need me, here's my cell phone number." He handed her an index card, lifted the box containing Cloud and her babies, and carried it out to his truck.

Zoe waved to him from his deck and returned to her laptop to straighten the manuscript and her notes in preparation for the meeting. When she put down the index card from Aidan, she found that it was more than his cell phone number. He had written, "Keep in mind that Kingston is heartless and a scoundrel. Don't lower your standards. Remember your dream to start your own small publishing house. Stay strong, Zoe."

Her boss, Larry Dennison, called to tell her that Kingston was going to be late. He tried to give her a pep talk, but mostly he reiterated, "Silence and a smile can go a long way."

While waiting, with the virtual meeting room still active in the background, she scanned additional pages of the manuscript and found more sections of bad writing.

She looked up and saw that her boss was doing the *New York Times* crossword puzzle. *Is he that prepared or is he planning to sit back and let me take the hits? Will he defend me or fire me?* She didn't know.

By the time that the virtual meeting started—one hour and forty minutes late—she had experienced a change in attitude. In the one-hundred minutes of worrying about what might happen, she had lost any enthusiasm for appeasing the self-centered author. She looked directly into his smug face and said, "The concept of your book is good. It will definitely sell, but not until you address the writing itself." She noticed the shocked look on her boss's face, yet Kingston seemed unaffected by her statement. So, she continued reading her notes. "You have good control of adjectives, but you overuse superlatives. The impression the reader will get is that you are an egotistic person, and I'm sure you don't want that."

Kingston stood and, doing so, filled the screen with his torso. She bit her lower lip to keep from laughing at this picture of the headless author, as it was such an appropriate illustration of who he really was.

"And this is the best editor you can give me?" he bellowed down at Larry Dennison.

Her boss, whose face indicated deep disappointment in her, said, "Zoe, you're fired."

The screen went blank. The meeting was over.

She didn't move. She looked at what Aidan had written. She had stuck to her standards. She had stayed strong. So why didn't she feel triumphant?

Zoe heard Aidan's truck tires against the crushed shells of his driveway. She put on a happy face and stood on the deck. "How'd they do at the vet's?"

He opened the car door and lifted out the box. "They all passed their checkups. The little girl is already trying to open her eyes. Figures. The two boys aren't even trying."

Cloud, who had been sitting next to the box, jumped out and ran to the wooded area.

Zoe was startled by this. "What will happen to the kittens if their mother goes away?"

"She's not going away. Like most mothers, she needs some alone time. Don't worry, she'll come back."

Zoe held the back door open for Aidan to enter with the kittens. She noticed that each kitten had a colored ribbon around its neck—one pink, one yellow, and one orange. "Do the colors mean anything?"

"It means we should name the kittens, so we don't need to keep calling them by colors."

"So, you're keeping them?"

"For now. At least until they're old enough to be neutered." He put the box down on the floor and turned his attention to Zoe. "How'd the meeting go?"

She held herself together the best she could. "I've been fired."

He wrapped his arms around her and held her close. Into her ear, he whispered, "I'm so sorry, Zoe. I should have stayed out of it. Just because I quit my job doesn't give me the right to suggest you put yours at risk."

"But you were right, Aidan. Being true to myself is what matters. And when I saw that arrogant look on Kingston's face, I told him the truth about his manuscript. I don't regret it, but I'm still in shock, I suppose. So, what do I do now?"

He stepped back just enough to look into her eyes. "Two roads diverged in a yellow wood, and sorry I could not travel both and be one traveler ..."

Zoe recognized the lines from a poem she'd studied in college. "Robert Frost."

"Yeah. On the subway ride to my apartment in Queens after resigning from Kingston's firm, I started questioning my resignation and considered going back to destroy the letter. Yet, I couldn't fathom spending my life in a day-to-day battle against my moral core. I felt lost. And then that Frost poem popped into my mind. I realized it was time for me to reevaluate my life. But that seemed such a daunting task. So, I bought a truck, packed up, and drove with no destination in mind. Somehow, I ended up here in Chincoteague. I figured I'd buy a fixer-upper and enjoy life in a small town near the water while I considered 'who I want to be when I grow up.' And that's my current plan."

"But we're different. I love being an editor. I didn't quit; I was fired. I don't see—" Her cell phone interrupted with the ding of a new message. She somewhat hoped it would be her boss, apologizing and telling her that she still had a job at Dennison & Harmon. But it wasn't a text from Larry.

Your building has been condemned. You must make an appointment to remove all personal property before July 15. National Guard will assist. Anything unclaimed will be thrown away. Use the link below to set your appointment.

She felt dizzy and reached for the kitchen island to steady herself.

"What's wrong, Zoe?"

She showed him the text. "It's the long story I mentioned yesterday. The apartment building where I was living was damaged by the collapse of a neighboring building. And now I have very little time to collect everything I own and find a new place to live."

He put his arm around her. "Let me help. How much furniture do you need to move?"

She shrugged. "None of it. The apartment came furnished. The building owner is the one to deal with that. All I need to gather are my linens, clothing, and personal stuff. Maybe twenty boxes at most, but what do I do with them?"

"Twenty boxes can easily fit in my truck," he said. "Tillie will be back in seven days and can take care of Cloud and her kittens. You and I could head to Philadelphia the day after her return and bring everything back here to Tillie's, temporarily. I'll help you take the boxes back to Pennsylvania, or wherever, when you have a new job lined up and a place to live."

"I guess that would work." She took a deep breath and then exhaled. "What am I going to do?"

"Nothing. Not for a while, at least. Spend the summer here, walk the beach, collect seashells, ride a bike. Relax. Enjoy time with your aunt."

Zoe was fighting to hold back tears. She didn't want to make the moment worse. "That would be nice."

"Exactly. Don't rush into grabbing the first job available until you have time to heal from this bad experience so you make the right decision. Okay, you love working with words. That doesn't mean that you have to work for a major publisher. There are other jobs that would satisfy that love, other careers that need your skills and talents. Give yourself time to figure out what you *really* want to do. Then, take the first baby step."

"Baby steps, huh?"

She looked around at all the improvements Aidan had made to his fixer-upper. Her reaction was a sharp contrast to her first impression, which had been based only on the unkempt outside appearance. She thought about his advice to take the time to self-repair before worrying about choosing another job. *Fix the inside before the outside.*

"It's your perfect chance to start fresh, Zoe."

He was right. She had the dream she had tucked away when she landed the job at Dennison & Harmon. Having watched some of her friends struggle to find an agent or get a manuscript past the circular file of a publisher, Zoe wanted to start a small publishing house where she could give new writers a chance. If ever there was a time to do this, it was now. She looked into Aiden's eyes. "Island Publishing of Chincoteague. What do you think?"

A warm smile spread over his face as he considered her question. "I'm thinking I'd be willing to wade into my old profession just far enough to help you get started—filing for your company's name, copyrighting your logo, drafting contracts."

Zoe stepped into his embrace. "But, Aidan, you don't want to be a lawyer anymore. You found a new path, one that makes you happy."

"I still have a passion for the law, just not corporate law. Being a handyman is rewarding, but pro bono work at Legal Aid would be more so." He kissed her check and whispered, "A journey shared is a journey worth taking."

"I like that," she said.

"Fortune cookie," he replied.

His deadpan expression made her laugh, and the more she laughed, the bigger the smile grew on his face.

Zoe shook her head. "Aidan, this is going to be one amazing adventure, isn't it?"

"We are going to take the one less traveled by," he responded. "And that will make all the difference."

Maybe We Will

At first, you avoided the beach, any beach, but especially this beach. Whenever possible, you drove the long way, down back roads, to get from Point A to Point B, adding thirty minutes or more to your travel time rather than chance a glimpse of the ocean—a difficult situation since you live in Dewey yet work in Bethany Beach, a town easily reached by simply driving south on Coastal Highway and over the Indian River Inlet Bridge. But your husband, Nick, eased you back from your self-imposed banishment from the inlet with short walks on other beaches—Lewes, Rehoboth, Fenwick Island, Ocean City—beaches with lifeguards, increasing time and distance a bit more with each outing.

You walked, but you kept your eyes busy searching for seashells or admiring the sea grass that protects the dunes. Anything but acknowledge the ocean. Your being here today at the North Indian River Inlet Beach, specifically Surfer's Beach, is a sort of final exam for which you're not prepared. In your gut, you know it's too soon to spread a quilt, raise an umbrella, and open the beach chairs at the very spot where these items stood a year ago when you witnessed the drowning of a child.

You often dream about children playing by the shoreline, digging in the sand, unattended. You watch them walking into the waves to collect water for their sandcastles. You imagine them pulled under and carried away by the undertow without a glance from the mother. Always, the dream ends with the sight of a lifeless little body lowered onto the wet sand, already too late for saving.

Shake the dream from your mind. Untie your beach cover-up and let it drop onto the quilt while Nick arranges the newly purchased beach chairs under the equally new umbrella. Try to ignore the reason for their newness, but you can't. The other chairs and umbrella were left behind, forgotten, abandoned, on the day of the incident.

Refuse the tears that try to form. Hide your face in the beach towel that hangs from the umbrella spokes until you feel Nick's arms surround you, folding you in like a receiving blanket. He whispers, "I'm here, honey. I'm here."

Lean your head back against his chest. "I know."

"Do you want to leave?"

You want to say yes, but shake your head no. Everyone's right. It's time to move on. You hadn't always hated the beach. You used to spend every free moment here. It's how you met Nick. He was your instructor for a paddleboarding class. Then your surfing buddy. Picture your beach wedding with the surfboards standing in the sand, creating the path for the ceremony. The two of you were the perfect match. But without the water these last thirteen months, it's been just two people sharing a house.

It's your fault. Fix it.

Turn inside Nick's embrace and slip your arms around his waist. Look into his eyes and give a smile that's just big enough to assure him. "I'm okay." Then, settle into the beach chair and close your eyes. Listen for the sound of Nick's movement—the soft crunch of the sand under the beach chair, followed by the sound of turning pages as he flips through his *Sports Illustrated*. Wonder if he's thinking about surfboards and if his muscles yearn to be in the ocean. You miss watching him ride the waves, dancing his board in front of the white tips of the breakers. Play the image in your mind like a favorite film clip—until memory breaks in like an annoying commercial. It takes you to that August day.

Remember a surfer, water sliding down his hair, screaming for an ambulance, carrying a small body to the shoreline. And a guy wearing an Iron Man Triathlon T-shirt, identifying himself as an EMT, and trying to resuscitate the child, all the while probably knowing it was already too late, but going through the actions dictated by protocol, waiting for an ambulance to arrive. You wonder now whether the protocol is really in place for the sake of onlookers, giving them hope, never letting them guess the awful truth.

You don't remember the child's face. Maybe the shade from the surfer shielded its details, or maybe you didn't want to see it. Instead, you remember looking past the crowd and watching an empty surfboard being tossed, wave to wave, and no one attempting to keep it from escaping out into the ocean. Recall watching the riderless board and the waves, while listening to the low conversations that floated through the air, bystanders assuring one another and themselves that the child would survive, that the staff at Beebe Hospital would be able to revive him.

Open your eyes to the sky and remind yourself that there is no child lying lifeless on the sand today. That was a different summer day, long gone. But the sound of the waves will not leave you alone. They tap on your mind like a toddler tugging on his mother's sleeve until a sudden desperate need leaps from deep within you, the illogical yet adamant need to make this torment stop. Spring from the chair and glare at the ocean.

Nick looks up from his magazine. "Beth? Are you okay?"

The caring tone of his voice deflates your anger. Soften your face. Lie. "Yes. A horsefly bit me." Hold out your arm, point to the nonexistent injury.

Nick kisses the spot three times, like a parent heals a boo-boo. But your boo-boo isn't healed. Something nags at your mind. You cannot erase the image of the little boy at the shoreline digging in the sand. You remember that he walked toward the water's edge to fill his bucket. You recall that your attention was drawn to the outline of a surfer paddling toward a building wave, the sunlight behind him turning him into a black cut-out. And then, it felt like time had stopped and the world was moving in slow motion like when a horrific event is shown in a film. But that time, it was real and, just like in the movies, you couldn't stop it from happening.

You remember that you couldn't get your legs to lift you from the beach chair, that you couldn't get your voice to call out. Remember watching the wave break high, close to shore. Remember blinking from one frame of the little boy with his plastic bucket to the next frame of no one there. Then the movie picked up speed, surfers rushing toward where the child disappeared under a wave.

Interrupt the movie before it plays over and over inside you. "Let's go for a walk." And, of course, Nick complies.

Hunt for seashells. You don't have to look up to know that Nick is watching you. Walk next to him, but not holding hands. Feel his concern and wish that you weren't such a burden to him. Wish for the *before* of your marriage. The bonfires on the beach, sipping beer from tinted soda cups, listening to the jamming of guitars, and the wild drunken dancing you never regretted.

Hand Nick a piece of broken shell shaped like an angel wing. He kisses your hand and places the shell in his pocket. Look for another one, another wing, and almost get one, but the undertow steals it away.

It's the game that the ocean almost always wins. All your life, you loved jumping waves, skim boarding, swimming past the breakers. Why didn't you see then that the ocean had this other side? A thief that takes seashells and surfboards and children.

The sound of high-pitched, gleeful squeals sends alarms through your body like electrical charges. Look up and see a family—parents under the umbrella unwrapping sandwiches from a picnic basket and three kids digging at the sand with their feet, giggling, seeing who can dig the farthest the fastest.

Nick grabs your hand and squeezes it. "Still okay?" His eyes worry.

"Sure." Smile. Pretend to be unaffected, calm, relaxed. Make yourself watch the children at play. Try to believe that not all children drown in the ocean.

Then, the smallest child runs toward the water.

His brother and sister are still kicking at the sand.

His mother and father are dividing the sandwiches onto plates.

Suddenly, you can't breathe. Perspiration floods your skin. Scream, "Joey!" and try to pull your hand from Nick's to run after the little boy. You must stop him. "Joey!"

Nick tightens his hand around yours with viselike pressure, grabs your waist with his other arm, and pulls you into him. "Stop it, Beth! It's not Joey."

In the background, hear the child's father call, "Benjamin! Not alone, remember?"

Feel air rush into your lungs, but the breath does not stop your mind from racing. In your memory, you see the face of a child in a baseball cap too large for his head, his little face smiling into the lens of your camera. Joey. Joey with Nick standing in the background, holding a surfboard at his side. Remember pressing the button on the camera, capturing what would be the final photograph of your son. Acknowledge that, on that August day, it was Nick paddling toward the breaker, and it was your son Joey building the sandcastle. Remember waving to Nick as he stood up on his surfboard. Remember turning to tell Joey to look at Daddy. Remember that the shoreline was empty. Your child was gone.

You're sliding from Nick's arms and you can't stop your awkward descent to the wet sand, don't want to stop, just need the earth under you.

Nick looks down in a silence that makes you ache for his embrace.

You say, "I remember."

He sits next to you on the sand. He starts to say something but stops.

Look into his eyes and see him as though for the first time since that horrifying day. Let your voice say the words again to know that you have actually said them. "I remember. Everything." Nick dressed in a dark suit. Nick helping you into a conservative black dress that that you don't remember ever buying, that isn't part of the clothing that hangs in your closet at home. Push through the fogginess that lingers in your mind. That black dress. There was never a black dress. "Nick, was there a viewing? Was there a funeral?"

"Yes."

Despite the pain that will stab your heart, confront the memory. Nothing. The images aren't there. "Why can't I remember it?"

Nick looks out at the horizon. "Honey, you weren't there."

Stare up at the pastel blue of the sky until your mind returns to a room whose solitary window looked out onto a gray city street. The salt air is replaced by the smell of Pine-Sol, and the seagulls' cries mimic the whimpering sounds that slip through the hallways of that sad building. "Oh."

Neither of you speaks. Together you look out at the ocean and watch a single surfer paddle past the breaking waves. Finally, get the courage to say, "I thought he was … safe … building sandcastles … safe. I should have—"

Nick cuts off your sentence. "Stop blaming yourself. It was nobody's fault. Or maybe everybody's fault." He wipes away water from his face—a mixture of sea spray and tears. Watch helplessly as wave upon wave of emotion breaks over him. Wait as his body shivers through locked-up feelings, until his breathing becomes regular again, and you know that he's reached a resting point.

You understand. These past months, he focused on your recovery, all the while not letting out his own grief. You know he'll never ride a wave again, not until he can forgive himself, as he has forgiven you, for not being able to save his son.

Move closer to him, your hip touching his, your arm around him, your head on his shoulder. Watch the surfer guide his board over the crest of the wave.

With his voice strong and resolute, Nick says, "We're going to be okay."

You feel the warmth of his body. Hear the rolling sounds of the ocean. And you think, maybe we will.

The Ethereal Shadows Left Behind

Before stepping out of the Congress Hall Hotel and into the bright May morning, Bella checked the supplies in her backpack—notebook, pens, camera, spare batteries, extra memory card, and, of course, a detailed map of Cape May on which she had circled a handful of must-sees. For several generations, her family had stayed at this historic hotel, famous as "America's First Seaside Resort." Her dad's side of the family claimed that one of their ancestors, Josef Zimmermann, had left New York with his wife, Gertie, and three children and moved to southern coastal New Jersey after accepting a job as a carpenter and furniture craftsman as this hotel was built.

Bella grew up hearing that story every summer until it had expanded so much that she doubted some of the details. But she wasn't here to reflect on family history, though she had dabbled a bit in genealogy after her parents gave her a subscription to Ancestry.com last Christmas with the suggestion that she find the truth about the Zimmermanns rather than continue accusing her Great Uncle Will of making it all up.

She was in Cape May this weekend as a photojournalist, collecting photographs and stories for her upcoming article to be published on *Beyond Sending Postcards*, a digital journal geared toward travelers who want to experience the soul of a travel destination. Her plan was to walk around, sauntering up and down side streets with no itinerary, looking for inspiration, and taking photographs of anything and everything that caught her attention. It was her version of brainstorming. Later, she would decide the focus for the article she'd eventually write.

Bella wandered from Carpenter's Lane to Ocean Street to Columbia Avenue to several of the less-traveled side streets, clicking images of porch columns, gingerbread scrollwork, gable-roofed dormers, latticework skirting, witch's-hat turrets, and fish-scale shingles. All the while, she took notes to remind herself where each photo was shot and what had prompted her to capture the image.

After more than an hour, her stomach reminded her that she hadn't taken time for a real breakfast; instead, she had gulped down a coffee and eaten a trail-mix bar in her hotel room. She longed for a relaxing lunch at an outside table of one of the eateries along Washington Mall and then a stop at Cape Atlantic Book Company for a romance novel, the naughtier, the better. It was her guilty pleasure and best escape from research and writing.

Just past noon, she was ready for that break. That is, until she turned a corner onto a short and narrow road with a missing street sign, probably an extension of another road except that she couldn't figure out which one. There were three houses on the left side and four on the right. Two of the houses on the right seemed to share a lot. One was visibly older than the other, although the newer one had been designed to replicate a Cape May "painted lady," the name given to Victorian houses with colorful exteriors.

Fascinated by the antique details, Bella stepped into the yard of one to take pictures of the house design as well as the flower-lined walkway that surrounded the house in a wavy, rambling way. As she leaned back to catch the sunburst structure under a gable, she sensed that someone in the neighboring house was watching her.

She quickly turned and stared back at the man who was standing on the porch. His clothing was summer-stylish Ralph Lauren. His face and brown hair, interrupted by an occasional silver hair, suggested his age was fortyish.

"I'm just taking photographs. Sorry if I'm intruding. Do you own this house, too?"

"For now. We couldn't get permission to build our house unless we guaranteed we'd let the old house remain. You a real estate agent?"

"No, I'm just—"

"Looking for a house to buy?"

"No." Bella shrugged. "Not that I wouldn't love to live here."

"Then why—"

Bella grabbed the chance to let him know how it feels to be interrupted. "I'm a photojournalist doing an article for a digital travel journal that focuses on the less obvious sites to see when traveling to a new city or country. Is it possible that I could walk around inside to take some interior shots? This house might be the center of my article."

He seemed reticent. "I don't know."

"It might encourage someone to buy it."

The suggestion worked, and the guy, who finally introduced himself as Taylor Brittingham, unlocked the front door of the old house. "Let me know when you're done.

And don't take anything."

"Aren't you coming in?"

But he was already sprinting up the steps of his front porch.

Once inside the house, Bella was surprised by what she saw. Unlike the historically preserved exterior of the house, the interior had been disrupted. It was clear that the previous owner, or the present one, had decided that prospective buyers would want a contemporary kitchen filled with stainless steel appliances and glass-doored cabinets. But for whatever reason, the installation stopped, and the effort to remove a wall had been covered up with white clapboard.

Bella turned her back to the new and faced the old, that is, the formal parlor on the other side of the narrow, wall-papered hallway. The centerpiece was a floor-to-ceiling, gray-stone fireplace with a heavy, oak mantel on which sat three knickknacks—a curved-wood clock that had not been wound lately, though its metal key lay underneath the slot where the mechanism would be turned, a blue-and-white, six-inch, china figure of a cat with the tip of one ear missing, and a tarnished-silver, photo frame with no picture beneath its cracked glass.

Nothing else in the room was of interest; the furniture was mostly twentieth-century replicas of nineteenth-century pieces that might impress potential buyers, but only if they knew nothing about antiques. Yet the items on the mantel were originals, despite the damage they'd endured over the years. She took several photos of each, then stepped back into the hallway. Its darkness was not due to lack of light, but because the walls were covered in wall-paper—heavy with deep, rich colors of burgundy, forest green, navy blue, purple, and only a minimal bit of creamy gold—and the steps and bannister were dark brown, most likely mahogany wood. Bella snapped photographs with and without the flash.

As she walked up the staircase, Bella once again felt she was being observed. Had the owner decided to shadow her as she explored the house?

"Taylor?" she called out, grabbing the bannister before turning around.

No one was there.

Then she had that same feeling, once again coming from above her. She quickly looked upward to the top of the staircase.

No one.

"This isn't funny," she said. "Who's playing this game?"

Silence.

Determined to gather enough visuals to support her article about historic Cape May architecture, she dismissed the fear that fluttered in her stomach. She continued up to the second floor, where she captured pictures of the three bedrooms and the bathroom, none of which had been modernized.

In the last room, she noticed a small door inside one of the bedrooms. When she opened it, she saw steps that led to an attic. The cobwebs that crisscrossed from wall to wall were at first daunting, yet they did indicate that no one had climbed to the attic in years.

Bella debated about whether it was worth the energy to capture images of the internal structures that held the witch's-hat turret and to explore whatever long-forgotten treasures may have been left behind as the house passed from family to family over the decades. Her own interest in ancestry spurred her on. Up the stairs she went, pushing aside the webs with her hands, grateful that she had long ago learned that cobwebs are webs that have been abandoned by the spiders who made them, and that dust was the only risk to knocking them down.

At the top of the stairs, she expected to find an old trunk or dresser filled with antique clothing, but the attic was empty. Still, she clicked away. It was during a closeup of one of the beams that she saw something etched into the wood: "Josef Jr., 1851." The fancy printed letters and numbers were carved by a careful hand, obviously done by someone with great skill.

Wanting to be sure that the markings showed up well in her camera's images, Bella took several shots, then descended the stairs from attic to second floor to ground level. She sat on the bottom step of the hallway staircase and clicked back through the photographs to see if any of them needed to be retaken.

The first image, which was the last photo she had taken inside the attic, puzzled her. She remembered focusing the shot on the name "Josef," but the image in her camera showed an additional name and date: "Jacob, 1856."

Bella rushed back to the attic.

There were indeed two names etched into the wood. How did she miss that? Attention to detail was central to her job as a photojournalist. *Perhaps it's too hot in this house and my imagination got away from me*, she thought. Yet, deep inside, she was doubtful.

Bella returned to the first floor and found her way to the enclosed back porch. She sat on one of the four, curved-bottom, bentwood chairs and rocked back and forth, enjoying the light breeze that moved through the porch screens. She reviewed the remaining interior photographs and they were exactly as she remembered them. It was a relief. All was well.

With her head cleared, Bella wanted one last visit to the parlor where she had photographed the fireplace and the objects on its mantel.

The sound of ticking stopped her in the hallway.

She inched toward the wide doorway of the parlor. Things were not as they were when she'd first stepped into that room. What she now observed was a room filled with true-to-period furniture, and everything was in working order. The clock was ticking. The cat's ear was intact. And an ambrotype photograph of a young girl was displayed under the clear, perfect glass of the polished silver frame.

Bella shook her head as though removing mental cobwebs from her brain in the same manner as having brushed away those that had clung to the walls of the attic access. Was she being pranked by the guy who was selling this house, or could the house be haunted?

The first explanation made no sense. The seller certainly wouldn't destroy the chance that Bella's article might bring a potential buyer. The only logical—if one can call it logical—possibility was that the house was haunted. But, if this were a haunted place, why had Bella felt no threat or danger? Rather, it was as though the house was trying to tell her something.

She felt compelled to examine the face of the young girl looking out from the framed photograph. The image seemed familiar to Bella, yet she didn't know why that would be.

A sound, not quite a voice, whispered, "Will you?"

At least, that's what Bella heard. Or thought she heard. "Will I what?" she asked aloud.

No answer.

She glanced down at her camera and checked the image of the attic beam. A third line had been added: "Willabella." It was a name! She didn't need to rush back to the attic, for she knew that the name would be there.

When she picked up the framed photo of the girl, her arms tingled. Memories rushed through her—some from Great Uncle Will, and some from what she found on that ancestry site. Josef and Gertie Zimmermann had two sons, Jacob and Josef, Jr. She wanted to dismiss this as coincidental; after all, those names were common in the nineteenth century. Yet, if the names carved on that attic beam were her distant relatives, then it would mean that the Zimmermanns had a connection to this house. Did Josef build this house as well as having worked on the Congress Hall Hotel?

Family. This time, the word was not a whisper. It came from inside Bella—an affirmation, perhaps, of the affinity she felt toward this young, blonde-haired, blue-eyed, little girl.

She returned the framed picture to the mantel and clicked open the Ancestry app on her phone. A new green leaf appeared in her family tree; Josef and Gertie had had a daughter, Willabella, born in 1860.

The name Willa had been part of the stories shared by her Great Uncle Will, the self-appointed griot of the family, but he claimed it as a cousin's name. Perhaps the full name, Willabella, had been abridged as the stories of their ancestors shifted from generation to generation.

She clicked the link in her family tree. A photo popped up on one of the branches. It was identical to the framed picture on the mantel. The digital image was identified as Willabella Zimmermann McGuire. Bella immediately recognized the name McGuire, her Great Aunt's maiden name.

"Home." The soft sound floated through the air, more melodious than the whisper had been.

"Home," Bella repeated.

The clock stopped ticking. The tip of the cat's ear vanished. The silver frame held cracked glass and nothing more.

Bella was never a fan of ghost stories, nor had she ever believed in seances or messages from beyond, yet she knew in her gut that she was meant to find this house. Or, should she say, for the house to find her? It had drawn her to it in the same way that people and places did as she traveled in search of a topic for her writing. She also knew that she was meant to be here beyond today.

But to purchase this house was most likely beyond her means. She had no idea how she'd get the money to buy it. Maybe she could ask her parents and her bother Jake to go in with her on the purchase, making it a family summer home.

Ultimately, their decisions didn't matter. Her mind was made up. Bella left the house, walked to the neighbor's porch, and asked, "How much are you asking for that Victorian?"

Taylor Brittingham, still seated there, responded with a price much lower than Bella had expected. What motive would he have for asking so little? She wondered if he had experienced the odd events inside the Victorian, or if he just wanted to dump it and be done with it, even if it meant getting below-market value

"Just remember that the old house can never been torn down," he said. "And you will be buying the house 'as is.' Don't expect me to fix things or care about anything that is awry." He handed her a clipboard that held a one-page document. "Sign this purchase agreement, contingent on your submitting proof of financing. I'd like to settle within ten days. I'm tired of the hassle of ..." He paused. "unlocking the door for gawkers who never intended to buy in the first place."

Bella perused the content of the agreement. It spelled out that she was agreeing to never tear down the house or bother him with buyer's remorse. Taylor Brittingham was being truthful. He wanted to be rid of his albatross and was willing to take a financial loss to do so.

As Bella watched him lock the door to the Victorian—Willabella's house—she thought, *This is what I've not seen written. Not a story of haunted Painted Ladies, but a story of ethereal shadows left behind.*

There it was: The title and focus for her Cape May travel story.

Puddle-Wonderful

Evie Peterson was overwhelmed. She stood in the great room of her newly purchased double-wide mobile home, surrounded by the remaining forty-seven unpacked boxes containing everything she owned—well, everything she chose to keep when she decided to move from New York to coastal Delaware. At least she had managed to get all her clothing into the closets and the chest of drawers.

She looked over the list she had created to connect box numbers with what was inside. Where should she begin? Her growling stomach answered. Kitchen supplies.

Evie ran the retractable cutter over the tape on boxes fifteen, sixteen, seventeen, and eighteen, and prepared to remove pots, pans, and baking dishes. While lifting out an iron skillet, she was caught by surprise when someone rang the doorbell.

Two men, both much younger than she (though she was never good at judging age) stood on her front porch holding a clear glass vase of fragrant lavender stalks and a pie with brown-sugar crumbles. She didn't know them. Of course, she didn't know anyone in the area except the real estate agent who sold her this mobile.

The tallest of the men, the one with wavy blonde hair and the greenest eyes she'd ever seen, spoke through the screen door. "Welcome to Pot Nets Bayside. I'm Jamie, and this is my husband, Neil." He gestured to the left with the vase. "We live next door."

Neil, whose dark-brown crewcut and deeper-brown eyes contrasted with Jamie's, stared down at the frying pan in Evie's hand. "Did we come at a bad time?"

Evie had forgotten that she was holding what could be misconstrued as a weapon. "Oh, my gosh. No. It's not a bad time at all. I was just unpacking my cooking items."

Neil held out the pie. "We come bearing gifts."

Jamie tagged on, "Yeah, we're either wise men very early for Christmas or we're the Greek guys who pushed the wooden horse into Troy." He laughed.

Neil rolled his eyes at his husband. "We hope you like Pennsylvania Dutch sour cream apple pie. It's Jamie's favorite, so I baked an extra one."

"I've never tasted a sour cream apple pie, but it sounds interesting." She opened the screen door to accept the pie but felt she was not being polite unless she invited them into her new home. "As you can see, I'm not unpacked yet, so the house is a mess, but you're welcome to come in. If we empty box seventeen, we'll have dishes so we can enjoy the pie together. Oh, and my name is Evie, the better version of Evelyn."

The guys came in, and while Jamie put the vase of flowers on the table, Neil helped Evie remove and wipe three dessert plates, three forks, and a knife.

"I haven't done much shopping yet, only a quick stop for essentials, so all I can offer you are bottles of diet iced tea," she said, as Neil cut into the pie and placed a piece on each plate.

While enjoying the pie, Evie was given a summary of the lives of Jamie and Neil. Both from New Jersey. Met at a party. Got married in Massachusetts, the first state to legalize gay marriage. Jamie was thirty-two years old; Neil was for-ty-one. Jamie was a home-staging professional who worked for several home builders and real estate companies, and Neil was the executive chef at Chez Vivre, one of the better restaurants in Rehoboth, according to Jamie. They moved here when Neil was recruited to head the culinary staff.

"Your turn to talk, Evie," Jamie said.

"Let's see. I lived in New York most of my life. I was employed as a copywriter for a marketing firm, where I worked until a few months ago when I became obsolete—the millennials had a new approach to marketing and were more adept at contemporary lingo. So, I retired. Early. My days of subway rides and long walks on the streets of Manhattan were becoming less fun and more dangerous anyway. It was time to get away from the city. I read an article about great places to retire, and Delaware with its tax-free shopping and off-season quiet sounded perfect. So, here I am."

Jamie glanced at the diamond ring she was wearing. "Married?"

"That's her right hand," Neil pointed out.

"So? She could be following the European tradition."

"No," Evie said. "This was my great-grandmother's wedding ring."

"*Ever* married?"

Neil jumped in. "Jamie! *Ever*? That sounds judgmental."

"Well, it wasn't intended that way," he explained to Evie. "I just want to get to know you."

"I wasn't offended in the least," Evie said. "I cohabitated with a coworker for a while, but we discovered that living together is not the same as merging lives. I liked my condo better when he and all his baggage—literally as well as figuratively—were out of my life."

"Well, get ready for a new beginning. This area is full of lovely people, a number of them retirees, too. And there are so many things to do. I'm not saying you have to hook up with a man. God knows, most men are pigs—excluding Neil and me, of course. In no time at all, you'll be surrounded by friends and activities. That's my promise to you as your next-door neighbor, and friend, if you'll have me."

Evie caught his enthusiasm. Suddenly, the piles of boxes didn't seem like mountains too high to climb.

The next week flew by. Jamie's work was contractual, so he had blocks of free time that he used to help Evie unpack the rest of her things. Then, he suggested the best ways to organize her double-wide and arranged and rearranged her furniture until both he and she were thrilled with the result.

To celebrate, Jamie and Neil planned a soiree at their home. The theme was "beach glamour," and everyone was to dress in summer-cocktail-party style. Jamie helped Evie pick out a dress from her closet—a sleeveless, black shift that had been her go-to for business parties. "As Billy Crystal said on *Saturday Night Live*, 'Dah-ling, you look maahvelous.'"

The guys held the party on their side deck and in the patio garden behind it. Tiny, white, Christmas lights decorated their trees and bushes, and garden lights surrounded the koi pond with its stone waterfall. Jamie's talents were everywhere in the design. Likewise, Neil's talents were displayed—and tasted—in the delicious hors d'oeuvres.

Everyone made her feel welcome and special. The

guys had made sure there were people Evie might enjoy getting to know—young and old, male and female, gay and straight—almost all with homes in Pot Nets Bayside. Before the night was over, she had been invited to yoga at the Lewes Senior Activity Center, lunches at Paradise Grill, and the TGIF wine blast that met at various homes.

Evie was loving her new life. No homesick longing for Manhattan. No regrets about retiring. Never a boring moment. But she wanted more than a social life. She *needed* to be *needed*.

After hearing about Sandpiper Cottage Adult Day Care, Evie answered the call to volunteerism. She started a Wednesday story circle. Each week, she had the center's clients choose a photograph from a magazine or suggest a topic. Then, she would improvise a story.

Her time at Sandpiper Cottage was joyous and fulfilling. When her Pot Nets friends tried to talk her into joining a Wednesday pickleball club, she declined.

When she mentioned this to Jamie, he asked, "What makes you happiest?"

Her face lit up as she remembered how great she felt every Wednesday after her story circle at the center. "Having a purpose beyond retirement."

"There," he said. "You found your answer."

As it turned out, keeping Wednesdays at Sandpiper Cottage was an excellent decision for Evie, though she didn't realize how excellent until a few weeks later.

That Wednesday, she met a new patient, Margaret Morgan, who was apparently in the middle stages of Alzheimer's. During the story circle, when Evie asked the group of six clients for story topics, everyone but Margaret offered suggestions. At the end of the fifth story, the woman hadn't yet looked up from her lap.

Before leaving the center, Evie asked a staff member about her.

"Ms. Morgan is new to our center, but not new to Lewes. She was born and raised here and has recently returned to live with family. Her dementia has reached the point where she can no longer live alone. I've heard that she had been a journalist in New York. Sad that a woman whose life was filled with words is losing her ability to communicate."

Evie understood and was determined to bring language back to Margaret, even if it would be only an observable acknowledgement of understanding words. She knew very little about Alzheimer's and guessed that her goal might not be in reach for this woman, but she would at least try.

And she did try. Evie started arriving earlier on her days of volunteering, at least an hour before story circle. She'd bring photographs of New York City—Broadway, Central Park, the Village. She'd have one-sided conversations in which she'd give sensory details about the place in the picture, or recount an event, or even tell personal stories about her own life in Manhattan. She noticed that Margaret's eyes would focus on whichever photograph she showed her. Although Margaret never said a word, she seemed to understand.

After two weeks of spending one-on-one time with Margaret, Evie tried a new plan to reach her. She printed copies of her New York photos and added words in large print along the bottom of each photo. Sometimes the words were simply descriptive, while other times she quoted well-known poems and song lyrics.

Immediately, she noticed a change in Margaret's interest. She reached for the photographs and held them. But she held one longer than the others. It was a colorful photograph of Central Park in the spring, on which Evie had printed,

> spring
> when the world is puddle-wonderful ...

When it was time to gather for story circle, Margaret still clasped that paper. And during and after stories were told in the group activity, she still held the photo of Central Park. Evie was pleased. She hoped that her adding a line from an e. e. cummings poem was the reason Margaret was connecting on some level with the juxtaposition of image and words.

The next week, when Evie arrived at the center with a portfolio of more photographs with words, she was surprised to find a man sitting next to Margaret.

He stood to greet her. Tall. Handsome. More than handsome. Sexy like a soap opera star. Jet-black hair with touches of silver at his temples. Crystal-blue eyes. Strong shoulders. And when he introduced himself as Drew Morgan, she just knew that this attractive man must be Margaret's husband. "Ms. Peterson, I wanted to meet you and thank you. I've seen a change in Maggie over the past week, and the staff has attributed that change to you."

Evie blushed. "Thank you. But I imagine she's just getting used to being here during the day." However, she also noticed that Margaret was still holding the picture of

Central Park.

"She kept that with her until she went to bed last night and I convinced her to let me lean it up against the lamp on the night stand," he said.

Evie opened her portfolio. "I have a new one for her. Times Square." The words printed under the photo were, "They say the neon lights are bright ..."

Margaret accepted the new photograph but put it under the Central Park one.

Drew's eyes moved from Margaret's hands to her face. "It looks like she's picked her favorite." He touched the photo. "Do you remember the time you and I rowed in the lake, Maggie?" he asked, but she didn't respond. Then he turned to Evie. "Would you mind if I stick around this morning? I'm usually busy during the week, but I cancelled my meeting today so I could meet you and observe how Maggie is handling this change from homebody to interacting with people who aren't family members."

Drew stayed for the story circle and listened to the stories Evie made up about the five topics suggested.

Again, Margaret didn't speak, but she did look up when Evie told a story about her fourth-floor apartment in New York and how the bedroom window looked out on a thin walkway, about five feet in width, that separated her apartment building from the next one, and how the guy who lived in that other building did vocal warm-ups every morning around eight a.m., and that she assumed he was an actor or opera singer or some other musical entertainer until she discovered he was a taxi driver.

Margaret laughed.

"You liked that story?" Evie asked, but the woman

returned to looking at the Central Park photo. Evie wondered whether calling attention to Margaret had been a bad decision.

After the group moved on to have lunch, Drew approached her. "May I take you to lunch?"

She assumed that he meant there at the center. "Oh, lunch is only for the clients."

He smiled. "Actually, I meant that I'd like to treat you to lunch at Kindle."

"The three of us?" she asked, nodding toward Margaret, who seemed to be listening.

"No, just you and me. This afternoon, Maggie will be picked up by my sister, Gayle, and her husband, now that they've returned from a much-deserved vacation."

Evie's first inclination was to decline, but she understood he was showing his gratitude. And probably, taking care of Margaret didn't give him much time to relax and chat with someone who responds. "Oh. Sure. That would be nice."

They drove separately because Drew was heading to a meeting afterward.

Lunch was delicious. They chatted about in-season vs. off-season in a beach town, something she hadn't quite experienced yet. He asked her where she'd grown up. When he learned she was a native Manhattanite, he asked her to talk about what life was like as a child growing up in New York. Each time she tried to move the conversation to his life, he turned it back to her. She wondered why he preferred listening to her rather than talking about himself.

When Evie got home, Jamie was sitting on his front porch, enjoying his four o'clock glass of chardonnay. "Hey, beautiful, you're later than usual."

"I had lunch with a client's husband." Before Jamie could make a smart remark, she added, "He wanted to thank me for my work at Sandpiper Cottage, but I think it was also because, as a caregiver to a loved one with Alzheimer's, he needed conversation time with anyone else."

Jamie nodded. "You better have left some room for dinner. Neil made beef wellington. And, because he was experimenting with flavors for French macarons, he made five different flavors—hazelnut, lemon, coffee, raspberry, and pistachio."

"Macarons? I'll make room, even if I burst."

He poured a glass of wine for her as she joined him on the porch. "So, where did you eat? What did you and ..." He held both hands palm up and waited for her to supply the name.

"Drew."

"You and Drew talk about? And does this Drew have a last name?"

She understood the confidentiality rule and that it meant never divulging the last names of client's families, so she said, "Don't know." Quickly, she moved on to recounting the lunch conversation and then told Jamie about Margaret. "I think she understands more than she's showing. But I'm not a doctor, so what do I know?"

"How long has Drew been married to Margaret?"

"I don't know. I didn't want to ask. And he kept the conversation centered on me."

"How gallant of him." Jamie tapped a finger against his

wine glass. "And what does he look like?"

She sighed and voiced her original reaction when she first saw Drew. "Talk, dark, and handsome like a soap opera star."

Jamie raised his eyes, and a smile crossed his face. "Girl, you know you want him."

He was right, but she hated herself for having feelings for someone with whom she could only be friends. "He's married, remember?" she insisted with every ounce of finality she could muster. In the future, if Drew stopped by Sandpiper Cottage, she decided that she would be polite but not personal, and she wouldn't accept any more invitations from him.

The next week, Evie returned to Sandpiper Cottage, but not as early as usual. She worried that Drew might be sitting with Margaret again and that she might not be able to conceal her attraction to him.

When she arrived, he was nowhere in sight. She felt relieved yet also disappointed and disgusted with herself for feeling that disappointment. But when it was time for story circle and she noticed that Margaret wasn't there, she panicked. Did her going to lunch with Drew upset Margaret? Would she never get the chance to continue her goal of bringing language back to her? Or did Drew sense she was attracted to him and know it would be improper?

Evie took out the photo she'd printed for Margaret: The Statue of Liberty, under which she had printed, "Her mild eyes command the air-bridged harbor ..." She may as well use it as the focus for today's storytelling.

The five regulars all wanted to say something about the famous landmark. They took turns mentioning remembered (or possibly made-up) memories of climbing the steps in the statue, of grandparents arriving in America, of patriotic celebrations at the VFW or American Legion, of studying "The New Colossus" (or what Louise called, "The Statue of Liberty Poem") in elementary school, and of watching fireworks around the statue on the Fourth of July. It was an easy session for Evie, as they were the storytellers and she was just a listener.

During the last, and particularly long, story of Independence Day in New York, everyone in the circle added extra details to the narrative. But Evie's attention was distracted when the door opened and Margaret rushed in, followed by a short, blonde woman, who was trying to keep up. "Maggie, wait."

But Margaret hurried into the vacant seat in the circle. She was out of breath and carrying a folder on which the Central Park photograph was displayed behind the clear front cover.

The other woman apologized for the late arrival. "I'm Gayle Harris, Maggie's sister. I always seem to be late. I have a lot to learn from our brother, don't I, Maggie?"

"Our?" The question popped out before Evie could stop it.

"Yes. Maggie is our big sister. I'm the middle child, and Drew is the baby of the family," she said. "Although, he'll kill me if finds out I called him that." She gave a quick wave. "I'll be back this afternoon—on time—I promise."

She had to ask, "So you'll be Ms. Morgan's transportation from now on?"

"Probably, since Maggie lives with my husband and

me. Drew pitches in from time to time, as he did while we were away."

As Gayle departed, it was time for the clients to have lunch. Still talking about the Statue of Liberty, all but Margaret left the room.

Evie sat next to her and handed her the new photo.

As Margaret slid it into her folder, Evie noticed for the first time that Margaret's only ring was a pearl set in rose gold, not a wedding band. Why hadn't she noticed that before? Why had she assumed Drew was Margaret's husband?

"Central Park is my favorite, too," Evie said.

Then, Margaret touched the cover of her folder and whispered haltingly, "In just spring when ... the world is mud-luscious the little lame ... balloon man whistles far and wee and ... eddieandbill come running from marbles and piracies and it's ..." She pointed to the words printed on that photograph: "spring when the world is puddle-wonderful."

Evie was shocked. "You can—"

"Sometimes. Even ... monkeys remember what they learn by rote," she said.

"Why haven't you let anyone know?"

"Because the words come and go. It's ... troublesome. And I don't like having my ... sentences ... finished."

Evie thought for a moment. "But if you give up *trying* to communicate, Ms. Morgan—"

Margaret touched Evie's arm and whispered. "Maggie. Please call me Maggie."

"Maggie. If you stop looking for the words, won't they leave sooner?"

She shrugged.

"Think about it," Evie said to her.

"Ms. Morgan," a voice called out. It was a volunteer at the center. "Lunch is being served. May I walk with you?"

Without answering, Maggie stood and went with the woman.

Evie remained for a few minutes. So many elderly people suffer from one form of dementia or other, and there was no guarantee that she wouldn't suffer that same fate at some point in her life. Then what? She didn't have a brother or sister or niece or nephew to be her caregiver. And worse, how would she feel when the words disappeared?

She understood Maggie's fear.

That afternoon, Jamie asked, "Why are you smiling like a Cheshire cat? What are you dying to tell me?

"Drew isn't married to Maggie."

"Maggie?" he asked.

"Yes, I learned that she wants to be called Maggie." She didn't share that Maggie was the one who made the request.

"So, if Maggie's not his wife, then he's available." Jamie held up his wine glass to toast.

Her smile decreased a bit. "That part I don't know. But at least, Maggie isn't his wife. I'm relieved that it won't make my relationship with her become uncomfortable."

Jamie was quiet, but she could see that he was plotting something. "You could ask Maggie if her brother is married. Oh, never mind. I forgot that she has Alzheimer's. That makes it difficult."

Evie almost slipped, almost revealed that Maggie had talked with her at Sandpiper Cottage earlier that day. She wanted so much to tell Jamie about the woman's secret, but it wasn't hers to share. Instead, she said, "Yeah, that's a problem."

"It would be easier for someone other than you to ask the question about whether he's married." Jamie's face lit up. "I have a plan. If he shows up at Sandpiper Cottage again, text me. I'll rush over and, after you introduce us, I'll invite him and 'his wife' to dinner at Chez Vivre, compliments of Executive Chef Neil Winters. And yes, reservations are typically required, but I'm sure Neil can make magic happen. At which point, Drew should either accept or admit to not having a wife. Just be ready for whatever answer he gives, okay? Deal?"

Evie held out her hand. "Deal."

The next week, Evie arrived earlier than her story group. More than ever, knowing Maggie's secret, she wanted to share more photographs with poems or lyrics. This time, it was a photo of the Queensboro Bridge, also known as the 59th Street Bridge, and words taken from the Simon and Garfunkel song: "Slow down, you move too fast. You got to make the morning last."

Maggie was sitting alone with her notebook on her lap. Her eyes were bright with anticipation. She saw the photo and smiled. Checking that no one was within hearing, she said softly, "I like the songs they wrote ... the two guys ... the tall one ... curly, tight, blonde hair ... other one shorter ... straight, dark hair ... someone and someone ..."

Evie remembered that Maggie had complained about having her sentences finished for her, so she waited.

"I had the record album. I can see their faces." She tilted her head.

"Simon and …" Evie started.

A big smile spread across the other woman's face. "Garfunkel." Then her face changed as though she had turned off the picture on a television.

Evie turned around to look.

Coming toward them was Drew. "Good morning, Maggie. My meeting was cancelled, and since you now live with Gayle and Steve, I don't get to see you every day, so I thought I'd stop by for a while." He sat next to his sister and looked down at the photograph in her hands. "What's today's photo, Evie? The Queensboro bridge? Great shot. New York always looks best in black and white."

He was so handsome. If only …

"Are you staying for the story circle today?" she asked, before realizing that it sounded like an invitation.

"If that's okay?" he asked, focusing on his sister, but not receiving any indication from her.

Evie wished Maggie would stop this charade of intellectual impairment, but she wouldn't wreck the connection they shared or her hope of getting her to reveal to her family that she could still communicate. So, she answered for her. "I think it would be great for you to stay." She glanced over at Maggie but couldn't read her expression. "If you'll excuse me for a moment." She stepped outside and texted Jamie. "Drew is here for the story circle. I just don't know whether you should come by."

He texted back. "I'll be subtle. Trust me."

Jamie arrived partway through story time, but stayed outside the circle, listening as Evie told a story about thunderstorms with lightning shooting across the New York skyline and standing on the bridge watching nature's fireworks. Afterward, he approached her with a small white pastry box, which he opened. "I come bearing gifts: chocolate mint macarons for you."

"They look delicious." She turned toward Drew "I'd like you to meet my next-door neighbor, Jamie. And Jamie, I'd like to introduce you to Drew, who is Margaret's brother." She almost called her Maggie, but that would open the question of why she stopped using the formal name of Margaret. "He's the gentleman who treated me to lunch last week."

"That was a kind gesture," Jamie said.

"The pleasure was mine. Evie has been helpful to my sister Maggie."

She noticed that Drew was sizing up Jamie, so she added, "Jamie and his husband, Neil, helped me settle into my new home." Drew's face relaxed. "And he and Neil introduced me to a great group of locals so I'd have a social life, too. I don't know what I would have done without them."

Jamie found an easy way in. "Speaking of social life, Neil is inviting a handful of people to a special treat—dinner at Chez Vivre—tomorrow evening. I think it would be wonderful if Drew and his wife would join us."

"I'm not married," Drew said.

Evie kept her face as uncommittedly blank as possible.

"Oh, I'm sorry," Jamie said. "I just assumed you were. Well, then, come solo or bring a date. Either way, I do hope you'll join us at the dinner."

Maggie, who had been silently listening to this exchange, nudged her brother and nodded toward Evie.

Drew looked at Maggie questioningly before saying, "Evie, do you already have a date to this dinner?"

"Not yet."

"Then will you be my date?"

She tried not to sound overly excited. "Yes. I'd love that."

As Jamie walked Evie to her car, he said to her, "It appears that I'm not the only Cupid around here. Looks like Maggie wants to see her brother with you."

The dinner party in the private dining room of Chez Vivre was more relaxed than Evie had expected. Jamie and Neil had invited two additional couples to keep Drew from recognizing the real reason for the dinner—getting Evie and him together. Neil had arranged to have the sous chef lead the kitchen that night so he could be free to enjoy his exclusive get-together.

The dinner conversation was entertaining. Drew seemed totally at ease with everyone, but especially attentive to Evie.

During the drive home, Evie sensed a tension in the car, but not a bad tension. There was the kind of electricity she remembered feeling when she met her first love during freshman year at college. That was years ago. No, it was decades ago. Jamie was right. It was time for her to find love again.

"Would you like to come in for some coffee?" she asked.

"That would be great."

Inside the mobile, he commented how spacious and beautiful her home was.

"That was almost all Jamie's talents," she said.

"He's quite a character, isn't he? And, more importantly, he's a good friend to you."

She carried the cups of warm coffee to the sofa and sat next to him. "More than good. He's probably my best friend."

"And a talented matchmaker," Drew added.

Evie felt embarrassed. She put down her cup. "I'm sorry."

He placed his hand on top of hers. "Why be sorry? I'd been trying to find a way to ask you out on a date ever since we had lunch the day I met you. If it hadn't been for Jamie, I'd still be trying to figure out how to let you know that I'm interested in seeing you without having to make excuses about coming to Sandpiper Cottage. I love my sister and would have stopped by to see how she was doing in day care, but you were the reason I canceled meetings on Wednesdays." He removed his hand and looked into her eyes. "Will it be okay for us to start dating?"

"Yes. I must confess that I was interested in you, too, but without Jamie, I guess I'd never have done anything about it."

"I needed that help, too, from Maggie."

Evie had kept Maggie's secret, so she wondered how much Drew had discovered. "Help from Maggie?"

He nodded. "She understands more than she pretends to. I'd been suspicious, but it wasn't until Jamie suggested I bring a date, that her nudge let me know for sure."

"You needed a nudge?"

"Let's just say I'm happy we got here." He leaned in and kissed Evie.

And suddenly, the world was puddle-wonderful.

A Sea Witch Festival To Remember

Since the arrival of her new bichon frise puppy nine days ago, Aimee never left home without Princess attached to her in a floral pet sling she'd bought on Etsy. When asked to explain why she took her dog everywhere, including to her workplace (thanks to a dog-friendly boss), she was quick with her defense: The puppy was bonding with its new "momma" and would be distressed if left alone too soon, and it was not yet apartment-trained. Besides, the puppy was being terrorized by a neighbor's cat who, being a bit old and senile (the cat, not the owner), often climbed onto Aimee's balcony to sing cat songs that sent Princess cowering under furniture.

With the puppy close to her heart, Aimee opened the door of Summer-by-the-Sea Day Spa, fully anticipating that Princess would become the center of attention.

Jan, the receptionist, squealed with delight and sang out, "Puppy alert!"

She may as well have called out "Fire!," because several stylists and aestheticians (as well as a woman wearing a hair-coloring cap with hairs sticking out from it) rushed into the waiting area to see the tiny bichon. There were the expected oohs and aahs, but too many hands reaching out to touch the puppy's soft, white hair sent Princess burrowing farther into the sling.

Aimee extracted her puppy from its hiding place and lifted it up so everyone could admire its sweet face. She said, "Don't be afraid, Princess," but the dog paddled its paws in the air as though trying to swim away. Of course, this delighted the ladies more.

Finally, Jan shooed everyone back to their stations, but she didn't follow her own directions. "Aimee, you must enter this little cutie in the Costumed Dog Parade!"

"The what?"

Shelby, Aimee's manicurist, interceded. "Jan, Aimee's only lived here since early spring. She might not know about the Sea Witch Festival."

The receptionist started to give the history of the festival, but Laura, who had just accompanied a client to the desk to check out, interrupted her. "Cut to the chase, Jan. Just tell her about the parade. Better yet, show her the album."

Jan reached behind the reception desk and brought out a scrapbook. "Most of us here at the spa are Yorkie lovers, so at the Sea Witch Festival each year we enter a float with our fur-babies in the Costumed Dog Parade."

Aimee noticed that the padded cover was a cotton print of Yorkies and that someone had added glittered letters that spelled "Sea Witch Cuties."

Nina, carrying a bowl of hair-color paste and a brush, returned to the reception desk. "Turn the pages, Shelby, so we can all look."

Shelby rolled her eyes. "It's not like you haven't seen these photographs a thousand times." But she immediately opened the book and flipped the pages, announcing each theme, as her colleagues provided commentary. She called out, "Zombies on the Beach."

Someone in the pedicure room squealed with delight.

"Ooh! That was our first parade. Remember, Laura, when your Bruno lifted his leg on Jan's Gigi?"

Jan squinched her nose. "It was disgusting. I had to remove Gigi's zombie dress, and she was forced to ride the float naked. She was inconsolable."

Laura's client, who was one step away from exiting the spa, called back. "Jan, dogs are always naked. Your Gigi was only upset because you overreacted."

"Maybe I would have been calmer if Laura had offered me her water bottle."

"It's not our fault you poured yours all over Gigi. Too bad you forgot what was in that bottle."

Jan acted indignant, but her eyes gave away her own amusement about the event. "Another reason Gigi was upset." She offered an explanation to Aimee. "Our bottles were filled with zombies on the beach. You know, fruit juices and three types of rum. We were younger then, and stupid, but luckily we weren't caught with the alcohol."

Laura dropped the credit card receipt from her client into a file box on the reception desk. "We're still stupid, but drinking made the parade day easier." Then, she whispered, "Gigi got a bit drunk from licking her paws, but it didn't harm her, thank God."

Jan nodded toward the photo. "That's Nina's Bubbles in the purple shirt, standing next to Shelby's Dandy Man in navy blue."

Nina smiled like a proud pet momma, but then excused herself to apply color to her very patient client.

Princess was getting restless, so Aimee returned her to the comfort of the sling and caressed the puppy's neck as the spa employees took their stroll down memory lane through the next few years of themes for their entries.

The second year, their float theme was "Hurricane Hits the Beach," with the dogs as fishermen on a tilting boat and manicurists dressed like fish. Secure in having gotten away with the drinks the previous year, they sipped rum hurricanes from plastic palm-tree cups.

Before leading her next client back to the manicure area, Laura gave a soft pat to Princess and said to Aimee, "We're not really a bunch of alcoholics, though those first two parades make us look that way. We stopped taking drinks to the parade after our manager suggested it wouldn't be a good idea to get arrested. Not good for the spa business, you know."

Shelby closed the photo album. "Anyway, now we drink *after* the parade. Usually at Nina's house because it has a great backyard where the dogs can run off their energy while their mommies get plastered."

Jan nodded at Princess, who was getting braver, poking her head out of the sling and looking around. "Really, Aimee, you must enter Princess this year."

Shelby disagreed. "There's not enough time for Aimee to get everything together for this year's parade."

That's all Aimee needed to hear—a challenge. "What exactly is 'everything'?"

"A costume for Princess and a matching costume for you. A parade float—"

Jan interrupted her. "She doesn't have to build a float. That's optional. It's just for crazy people like us who are die-hard, Sea Witch fanatics."

"But, this late in the month, there won't be any decent pet costumes available. The Halloween Store only had dog tutus left when I stopped there yesterday to get decorations for the spa. And by now, Walmart and Kmart will be picked over. Jan, you're setting Aimee up for failure."

Failure? Aimee was now more determined than ever to enter Princess in the dog parade. And win, of course! "Shelby, I appreciate your effort to protect my pride, but I accept the challenge."

As a newbie to the Rehoboth area, Aimee had an advantage she didn't share: She had a college degree in theater and sewing skills (sort of). Okay, her sewing talents consisted of knowing how to cut fabric and operate a sewing machine, as long as the item didn't require buttonholes or a zipper. She had never gained those skills, no matter how many times her costume-designer friends told her that the sewing machine can perform both techniques with very little assistance. Her usual response was, "Isn't this why Velcro was invented?"

Though the women of Summer-by-the-Sea Day Spa wouldn't reveal their theme for this year's entry, Aimee was eager to compete against them. And, by the time her nails were dry, she was filled with inspiration and determined to impress everyone with her own creativity. Best of all, she had a plan. Although she wasn't prepared to take on the task of making a parade float, she knew she could knock out a costume easily, even though the Sea Witch Festival was only two weeks away. Two weeks?

Being at least a bit realistic about the timetable, Aimee rummaged through her storage closet at home, dragging out Rubbermaid containers (damaging her newly applied nail polish in the process) until she found the ones labeled "costumes." She hadn't been in a show for years, but she had saved some costumes as a just-in-case-I-ever-do-a-show-again or if-I-ever-get-invited-to-a-masquerade-party, neither of which was likely. She had left all her drama buddies back in Richmond when her job brought her here to coastal Delaware. So far, Princess was her only social companion.

She spread the costumes across the floor. A fairy godmother gown from *Cinderella*. A nun's habit from *Nunsense*. A cowgirl dress from *Oklahoma!* The Daisy Mae dress from *Li'l Abner*. An Elizabethan gown from when she and her last boyfriend (emphasis on "last") worked at a Renaissance festival. These five costumes all had possibilities; the big decision was which one would provide the best (and easiest) companion piece for a puppy.

Princess, who had been terrorized by the large Rubbermaid containers, emerged from behind the ottoman. She sniffed each costume, then curled up on the Renaissance gown.

Aimee took this as a sign. "Good girl, Princess!"

Being new to southern Delaware, Aimee googled local fabric stores. She was unpleasantly surprised to find only one fabric store, and it was forty-five minutes from her apartment in Lewes. She turned to Princess. "I'd drive all the way to Richmond if it would get you the best Renaissance costume ever."

She secured the puppy into the doggy seat and drove to Dover with visions of brocades and lace. However, when she (and Princess, now transferred to the pet sling) arrived at the fabric store and checked the pattern books for dog costumes, there weren't any Elizabethan costumes for pets.

Big surprise!

But that didn't dissuade Aimee. She checked the doll clothing patterns and found a blouse and vest intended for teddy bears. This could be doable except that it lacked the stiff, curving, clown-like collar that Renaissance nobility wore around their necks. At first, she couldn't remember the name of that collar. When it finally popped into her head, she laughed. *Ruff*! How appropriate that a dog would be wearing a costume piece that sounded like a bark.

She found directions on the Internet for making a ruff; they seemed easy enough. The article suggested buying two yards of wide grosgrain ribbon. Of course, the directions were for a human's neck; Princess wouldn't need that much. Still, Aimee bought a whole spool of two-inch grosgrain, figuring she'd need the extra yardage for all the mistakes she might make.

Might make? Would make! She recalled her past misadventures in costuming. There was the semester at college when she was an intern in the costume shop, and after wrecking one too many sewing projects, she was demoted to sweeping up thread and fabric pieces.

After stressing over which brocade and what color (royal blue or regal purple), whether to use white lace or ivory, and if rhinestones would show up better than pearls, Aimee heard Princess whining, as the puppy did whenever she needed to pee. Aimee had already learned that, with puppies, seconds count in avoiding mishaps. So, she made the quick decision to buy some of everything. She informed the fabric cutter of the amounts needed and rushed Princess out of the store to a small plot of grass nearby.

When Aimee returned, the cashier was waiting to total

her purchases: one spool of three-inch grosgrain ribbon (at a shocking $9.99 per spool), one yard of royal-blue brocade with silver accents and one of deep, regal purple with gold accents, several yards of lace, strings of pearls for the bodice, and one yard of bleached muslin and one of cotton gauze (she had been unsure which would look best and be easiest for making a blouse for the dog). Then there were spools of thread in various colors, as well as snaps, hooks and eyes, and her beloved Velcro to give her several choices for closures (but no zippers or buttons). The cost for this doggy costume added up to a whopping $168.84. She was wide-eyed but, of course, she couldn't change her mind now; cut fabrics are never returnable.

Back at home, she set up the sewing machine and settled in for the challenges that awaited. Six hours later, with pattern pieces, fabrics, and notions spread over the kitchen counter, Aimee acknowledged that she was in over her head. *The Late Late Show with James Corden* was signing off, and she planned to do so, too. Tomorrow was a workday, and she couldn't be less than perfect in her job if she wanted her boss to continue letting her bring Princess to the office with her every day. So, with Princess in the doggy bed, Aimee set the alarm clock and fell into bed in the clothing she'd worn all day.

The next week and a half were filled with cut, sew, try on the dog, rip out the stitches, correct the seam marks, adjust the pins, sew, and try on the dog, until the blouse and the basic bodice with its peplum were complete and perfect in size. She bought pliers to make grommets so the bodice could lace up (historically accurate, if dogs had worn bodices during the Renaissance). Then, she hand-stitched decorative beading until every one of her fingers was bandaged. She saved the toughest job for last: making the ruff. Actually, ruffs. She built three versions of the doggy ruff until she finally got one that looked authentic and fit Princess's neck. Done! And two days before the Sea Witch Festival.

Two days? She stared at the calendar. Two days. Visions of parade floats danced through her mind (apologies to the poet who created "The Night Before Christmas"). She wondered if Walmart had a Radio Flyer wagon at a good price. Or, maybe she could borrow a plant cart from Lowes.

The neighbor's cat yowling on the balcony sent Princess scurrying under a pillow on the sofa. That was enough to pull Aimee back to reality and the realization that she was too tired to add a parade float this late in the game. After all the money she paid for the materials for Princess's costume, she was hesitant about investing any more of her paycheck, especially since the resulting float might be a disaster. On her resume of drama aptitudes, her carpentry skills were lower than her sewing talent.

The Sea Witch Festival weekend arrived with beautiful autumn sunshine. The weather was warm and sunny enough to pass for late summer. For a moment, Aimee wished she'd chosen the Daisy Mae costume with its off-the-shoulder gauze top and shorty-short cotton skirt. It would have been much better for a hot day than the heavy materials in the Elizabethan gown. But she was so proud of the clothing she'd made for Princess that she was willing to swelter in the bright sun.

Excited for Princess's debut in the Costumed Dog Parade, Aimee's hands shook a bit as she dressed the puppy. Princess was not cooperative. As soon as Aimee got one paw into the blouse and reached for the other paw, Princess removed the first one. "Princess, baby, you are going to have to get over it. Momma doesn't have an ounce of patience to spare today, okay?"

Eventually, the blouse was snapped into place, along with the Elizabethan ruff, but the puppy was not happy about it. Princess lay on her back and tried to rub the blouse off. When that didn't work, the puppy scampered from the room as if it could outrun the costume. Aimee had not considered that the dog might need to be introduced to clothing a little at a time. Oh, well, too late now.

Aimee ran after Princess, following her into the master bedroom, where the dog disappeared under the bed far enough that her human couldn't reach her. The puppy wouldn't budge, even when offered her favorite chew toy. Aimee said, "I don't have time for this!" and she meant it. She knew it wouldn't be easy finding a parking spot in Rehoboth.

Figuring it might give the puppy time to come out on its own, she put on her own costume and interwove her long hair into a single French braid. The tactic worked. While dabbing on some makeup, Aimee felt a lick on her ankle. When she looked down, Princess was sitting on the floor, still wearing the Elizabethan blouse.

"Good girl!" She put the puppy on the bed and added the second piece of the Renaissance doggy costume—the bodice with its peplum. She didn't know whether it was easier because the dog had given up or because Aimee had been smart enough to make it a step-in with Velcro to hold it closed while she laced the back. She attached the ruff. Finally, Princess looked like a princess.

Aimee carried the puppy to the car and headed toward Rehoboth Beach. Her stomach churned the whole time. She endured bumper-to-bumper traffic down Route 1, then several tours of the downtown streets before she found a parking spot.

"We're here!" She lifted Princess from the car seat, and it was then she realized she had left the pet sling at home. Panic time! Of course, she could carry the puppy in her arms, but she didn't know if that was allowed in the costume contest. Then, she remembered the collar and leash she kept under the doggy car seat for emergency pee stops. It was thin and fit under the Elizabethan ruff. "Time for your debut."

Princess seemed confused and started frantically smelling the concrete sidewalk as if searching for something. Aimee realized what was happening: The puppy associated that leash with peeing and was looking for grass, not an easy find on Rehoboth Avenue. In the meantime, a group of costumed children had spotted them and rushed over to touch the puppy.

The bichon, more frightened of children than of the cat on the balcony at home, tried to climb up Aimee's dress as an escape. Aimee lifted her dog and (as sweetly as possible) made up an acceptable lie for the children. She explained that their Halloween costumes were so great they had scared the puppy. The kids beamed with pride, and Aimee hurried away before the children could realize that some of their costumes weren't supposed to be scary.

When she arrived at the judging station at the north end of the boardwalk near the Henlopen Hotel, the roped-off parking lot was filled with costumed adults, costumed children, and costumed dogs, while parade floats of various sizes had been positioned on the boardwalk. The whole event was overwhelming to both Aimee and her dog. The puppy was terrified by all the other dogs dressed in Halloween costumes.

Aimee found a clear space and lowered Princess to the ground. Immediately, the dogs nearest to them pulled at their own leashes so they could sniff the puppy. In an act of self-preservation, Princess rushed under Aimee's skirt to hide. Unfortunately, this caught the attention of a Great Dane dressed as Superman. The young child holding Superman's leash lost his grip, and Superman attempted to find Princess under Aimee's skirt as though the little bichon were a toy. Aimee tried her best to stop the Great Dane, but this resulted in Aimee losing her balance, falling backward, and knocking down a judge, who happened to be walking past at that moment. Her fall also revealed Princess, who was sitting on the ground and looking up into the monstrously large face of Superman. Aimee freaked out. "Oh my God! My puppy!"

But her fears were unnecessary. The Great Dane simply lowered his head and licked the bichon. It seemed that Superman only wanted to meet Princess. The child's father rushed over to retrieve the wayward Dane. "I'm sorry, Miss. Our Sassafras is a loving dog. He does this stuff all time. He doesn't realize how big he is."

Before Aimee could accept the apology, the judge reprimanded the man. "Your dog is too big and too powerful to be controlled by your son. If the dog gets loose again, we'll be asking you to leave the contest and not participate in the parade."

From the far end of the staging area, someone called out, "Aimee!" Shelby and the other girls from the spa were waving to her.

Aimee lifted Princess and slipped through the crowd, passing a golden retriever Batman, a trio of dachshunds dressed as the Three Musketeers, a miniature poodle Tinker Bell, and dozens of other pooches in every costume imaginable. Finally, she reached the Summer-by-the-Sea Day Spa float.

"Ta-da!" Shelby said, with her arms open toward their float, indicating their theme for this year's contest: "Hawaiian Hula Eruption." The float contained a tall volcano with smoke coming up from its core and four Yorkies in hula skirts and bright leis made of silk flowers. Aimee acknowledged she was outdone.

Shelby whispered to her, "Wait until the judging starts. We have a surprise built into our float this year." Before she could give the details, a loudspeaker clicked on, and everyone was instructed to line up for the judging. "Stay close by, Aimee. You'll want a front-row seat for this."

The judges walked past the line of people and pets without even looking at Princess. "Hey!" Aimee held her puppy higher. "You missed my puppy!"

A woman next to her gave her a gentle nudge. "Don't bother. They'll come by again. The first part of judging is focused on the floats." When Aimee sighed, she added, "Don't worry. The floats are a separate category."

What a relief. Aimee and Princess wouldn't be competing against Shelby and that amazing island float with its smoking volcano.

As instructed by Shelby, Aimee kept her eyes on the spa float, watching as all nine of the judges prepared to score it.

All of a sudden, a rumbling sound, like a Harley motorcycle starting, was heard above the general noisiness and chatter.

The crowd got quiet.

The noise increased.

It seemed to be coming from the spa float.

Abruptly, something inside the volcano exploded. Flames and pieces of blackened Styrofoam shot into the air.

Aimee held tightly to Princess as the four hula-skirted Yorkies jumped from the float and ran in every direction, pursued by the spa ladies. Shelby's Dandy Man jumped into a woman's Something Comfortable shopping bag, digging so hard to find a hiding place that he tore through the bottom of the bag, scattering the lingerie. Then, he ran off toward the boardwalk with a bra dragging behind him. Shelby, ready for anything, handed the woman a gift certificate to the salon and a promise to return the bra as soon as she could catch up with her Yorkie. Bruno had jumped into an escaping baby stroller, causing the young mother to make an abrupt stop in her flight away from the commotion; Laura screamed for her to grab Bruno, but the Yorkie jumped out and ran away, with his owner running behind. Gigi and Bubbles had disappeared in the scattering crowd, so Jan and Nina split directions and called both dogs' names.

But the Yorkies weren't the only pets in escape mode.

Other dogs, also spooked by the sound of the explosion, pulled away from their families and took off, dragging their leashes behind them. Everyone was grabbing children, while screaming dogs' names and distancing themselves from the Hawaiian Hula Eruption float, where an employee from the nearby hotel was trying unsuccessfully to get a fire extinguisher to work, all the while cursing so loudly that mothers were clamping their hands over the innocent ears of their children.

The sound of a fire truck added to the din, and the responders were welcomed with cheers, as everyone who was still in the staging area of the small parking lot moved back against the buildings to let the truck through. In the process, Gigi and Bubbles were spotted together, shaking as fiercely as only small dogs can. One of the spa clients, recognizing the dogs, lifted them, consoled them, and scanned the crowd for any sight of Jan and Nina. Spotting them near the flaming float, she screamed out their names, and the receptionist and stylist rushed toward their dogs.

The firefighters saved the day. Once the fire was put out and the commotion settled down, most of the dogs had been reclaimed and the crying children calmed. It was decided that everyone was a winner this year and that the parade down the boardwalk (minus the hula float) would commence.

Shelby and her coworkers were embarrassed about the mishap, but the judges assured them that they could participate in the parade anyway. So, the four hula-skirted Yorkies (and their Hawaiian-shirted humans) accompanied the Elizabethan bichon (and her Renaissance human), and together they walked in the Costumed Dog Parade, waving to the crowd that had gathered on the benches and on beach chairs set up along the parade route. As they passed each block, people clapped and shouted, "There they go—this year's entertainment," "What a bang-up job," "You guys are hot," and so forth.

Halfway down the boardwalk, a little girl from the sidelines pointed to Princess. "Look, Mommy, the queen's dog has a best friend." Sure enough, Princess was walking side by side with Nina's Bubbles.

At that, Jan sang the first line of the Don Ho song "Tiny Bubbles" loud enough that Aimee wondered if they had been telling the truth when they claimed sobriety for the parade.

Shelby winked at Nina. "Maybe next year, we can find a way to add a bichon on our Yorkie float. Perhaps we'll have Marilyn Monroe and four dancers. We'll call the float 'Diamonds Are a Girl's Best Friend,' that song Monroe sang in *Gentlemen Prefer Blondes*."

Aimee shook her head. "On your float? I don't know …"

Nina laughed. "Don't worry. The judges informed us that we can't ever have any special effects on our float again or we'll be banned from the contest. Forever. Lesson learned, right, girls?"

Jan pretended a pout. "First they take away the alcohol, and now they take away the explosives. What next?"

Nina comforted her. "I hear that there are adult beverages waiting for us on Olive Avenue. And, if you want to take your chances with more fireworks, I think my William has some sparklers in the garage. He's been chilling frozen piña coladas and prepping munchies all morning for us. That includes you, Aimee. You're invited to my house after the parade."

Aimee couldn't have had a better introduction to the

Sea Witch Festival. Princess could go home as a winner, though no one back in Richmond would hear that every doggy participant had been given that title, and Aimee was invited to her first party in Rehoboth. Not a bad day at all.

As she sipped the heavily-liquored piña colada, her new buddies were already brainstorming next year's parade float.

"So simple. Nothing but a set of stairs," Jan said.

Nina's husband, who was the master builder for them, laughed. "We could recycle some of the scorched wood from this year's fiery explosion."

"Sure, the float will be easy. It's the costuming we need to worry about. Technically, our Yorkies need to wear tuxedo jackets," Shelby complained. "Where will we find tuxes for dogs?"

Aimee had the answer. "I can make them."

Everyone looked over at her and then at Princess. "You made that costume?" Jan asked.

She nodded. "I took costuming in college."

Applause broke out, and Jan held up her glass to make a toast.

"Wait!" Nina rushed into the house and returned holding a red velvet dog collar studded with cubic zirconia. "Bubbles will lend Princess her royal collar."

They raised their glasses. "Until next year!"

Nancy Powichroski Sherman

Nancy Powichroski Sherman is a storyteller. Born and raised in Baltimore, MD, she dreamed of living near the Atlantic Ocean. After over forty years of teaching, she and her husband, Matthew, moved to coastal Delaware near Rehoboth Beach and became pet parents of two bichon frises, Pookie and Zoey.

Nancy's first collection of short stories, *Sandy Shorts*, was awarded a regional first place by Delaware Press Association and national first place by the National Federation of Press Women (2015). Her award-winning short stories have also been published in several anthologies: *The Beach House, Beach Love,* and *Beach Pulp* (Cat & Mouse Press); *Rehoboth Reimagined* and soon-to-be-released *Scenes: A Collaboration of Coastal Writers and Artists* (Rehoboth Beach Writers Guild); and *The Divine Feminine: An Anthology of Seaside Scribes*, *She Writes: Visions and Voices of Seaside Scribes,* and soon-to-be-released *Seaside Scribes: An Anthology of Women Rising* (Salt Water Media). With her home in coastal Delaware near Rehoboth Beach and Lewes, her stories are influenced by life in beach towns.

Nancy and her parents at the beach.

If you enjoyed *More Sandy Shorts*

Sandy Shorts

What do you get when you combine bad dogs, bad men, and bad luck? Great beach reads. You'll smile with recognition as characters in the stories ride the Cape May-Lewes Ferry, barhop in Dewey, stroll through Bethany Beach, and run into the waves in Rehoboth. Stories are grouped into sections labeled "Sunny Days," "Shifting Sands," "Stormy Skies," and "Starry Nights," according to their mood.

The Sea Sprite Inn

Jillian has lived through more than her share of tough times, but leaps at a chance to reinvent herself when she inherits a dilapidated family beach house. Now, along with bath towels and restaurant recommendations, she offers advice, insights, and encouragement—with a side dish of humor—as owner of The Sea Sprite Inn in Rehoboth. As guests come and go, each with unique challenges and discoveries, Jillian learns to trust her instincts and finds a clear path to her future.

Rehoboth Beach Reads Series

These anthologies are jam-packed with just the kinds of stories you love to read at the beach. Each contains 20-25 delightful tales in a variety of genres, authored by many different talented writers.

Eastern Shore Shorts

Whether you're in the heart of the Eastern Shore or the Eastern Shore is in your heart... Characters visit familiar local restaurants, inns, shops, parks, and museums as they cross paths through the charming towns and waterways of the Eastern Shores of Maryland and Virginia.

www.catandmousepress.com

44904090R00137